TEN MODERN

SCOTTISH STORIES

Ten Modern
Scottish Stories

Selected with an Introduction, Talking Points and an
Appendix on the Art of the Short Story

by

ROBERT MILLAR, M.A.
Moray House College of Education

and

J. T. LOW, B.A., M.Litt., Ph.D
Moray House College of Education

HEINEMANN EDUCATIONAL BOOKS
LONDON AND EDINBURGH

Heinemann Educational Books Ltd

LONDON EDINBURGH MELBOURNE AUCKLAND TORONTO
HONG KONG SINGAPORE KUALA LUMPUR NEW DELHI
NAIROBI JOHANNESBURG LUSAKA IBADAN
KINGSTON

ISBN 0 435 13545 7

Published by
Heinemann Educational Books Ltd
48 Charles Street, London W1X 8AH
Printed Offset Litho and bound in Great Britain by
Cox & Wyman Ltd, London, Fakenham and Reading

Contents

Acknowledgements

The editors and publisher wish to thank the following for permission to reprint the stories:

1. Faber and Faber for 'The Kitten' by Alexander Reid from *Scottish Short Stories*.
2. Rupert Hart-Davis for 'The Bike' by Fred Urquhart from *The Ploughing Match*.
3. The Hogarth Press for 'A Treading of Grapes' by George Mackay Brown from *A Time to Keep and Other Stories*.
4. Victor Gollancz for 'Home' by Iain Crichton Smith from *Survival without Error*.
5. Ian Hamilton Finlay for 'The Money'.
6. Robin Jenkins for 'Flowers'.
7. Nora McIlhone for 'Jenny Stairy's Hat' by Margaret Hamilton.
8. A. D. Peters and Co. for 'Sealskin Trousers' by Eric Linklater.
9. The Estate of the late Neil M. Gunn for 'Art's Wedding Present' from *Young Art and Old Hector*.
10. Hutchinson & Co. for 'Forsaken' by Lewis Grassic Gibbon from *A Scots Hairst*.

Introduction

The purpose of this volume is to show something of the scope
and range of the Scottish short story of the past three or four
decades – the mid-twentieth century. In the nineteenth century
and early twentieth Scottish story-writing was developed by
writers like Scott, Galt, Hogg, Stevenson, MacDonald,
Cunningham Graham, Crockett, Barrie, Neil Munro and
John Buchan. We hope that this present collection will go
some way towards demonstrating that the Scottish writer
has continued to practise, develop, and experiment with the
craft of the short story.

The stories selected represent different aspects of life in
different settings in Scotland urban and rural, picturesque and
sordid. It is not important that the settings should be obviously
or typically Scottish. What is more important is the quality
of the experience described: these stories reflect facets of the
Scottish mind and character that are seen to have a universal
significance in their contemporary context. Hard realism
jostles with human sympathy and understanding in Margaret
Hamilton's 'Jenny Stairy's Hat', Fred Urquhart's 'The Bike',
and Lewis Grassic Gibbon's 'Forsaken'; beneath the apparently
peaceful rural settings of 'The Kitten' and 'Flowers' there
lurks sharp criticism of man and society; and in Neil Gunn's
story of the illicit still, as in Linklater's story of the seal-man,
some kind of constructive philosophy of life is sketched. In
Iain Crichton Smith's 'Home' the mental attitudes of people
who have changed their social status are presented with great
irony and satire. 'A Treading of Grapes' and 'The Money'
are more humorous studies of human beings in all their
pomposity or officialdom: the first is also remarkable for its
tripartite structure and the second for its apparently artless
method of story-telling.

Indeed, these ten stories exemplify different methods of structure and technique. Both George Mackay Brown and Lewis Grassic Gibbon are seen as experimenters superimposing on a basic text or legend contemporary scenes or characters. Robin Jenkins and Alexander Reid use a dramatic method in building up to their moments of revelation or high climax. In Margaret Hamilton's story there is something of the technique of the novel in the unfolding of character and the weaving together of episodes. Neil Gunn uses a finely balanced combination of talk and action, episode and reflection, to present the universal truths behind the story of Art and Hector. 'Art's Wedding Present' is actually an extract from a novel but seems to us to have the quality of a short story, being completely developed and unified within itself. The ironic effect of Iain Crichton Smith's story depends on the superimposition of the opulence of the couple upon the memory and reality of their earlier poverty. To become aware of the structure and technique is not to destroy the effect of the narration: it rather helps us to appreciate the power and deeper meaning.

There is represented in this collection a variety of styles and methods, from the wonderfully simple, terse, and economical force of Alexander Reid's 'The Kitten' and Robin Jenkins' 'Flowers' to the more complicated techniques used by Iain Crichton Smith and George Mackay Brown. The main accent is on the practicalities and problems of modern life as in Fred Urquhart and Margaret Hamilton; but there are glimpses of the romantic, the idealist, the supernatural, in the work of George Mackay Brown, Lewis Grassic Gibbon, Neil Gunn and Eric Linklater. As for language, the modern English idiom tends to predominate; but in many of the stories the Scottish quality is unmistakable – in word, idiom, or attitude. Occasionally, notably in the work of Neil Gunn, one hears the lilt of a Gaelic rhythm.

Talking Points – sets of questions for discussion on the

themes, structure, and the human condition illustrated – are attached to each story. These, it is hoped, will encourage readers to study the art and technique, the social problems and the commentary on life, that lie behind the modern Scottish short story.

R.M.

J.T.L.

Alexander Reid (b. 1914)

THE KITTEN

The feet were tramping directly towards her. In the hot darkness under the tarpaulin the cat cuffed a kitten to silence and listened intently.

She could hear the scruffling and scratching of hens about the straw-littered yard; the muffled grumbling of the turning churn in the dairy; the faint clink and jangle of harness from the stable – drowsy, comfortable, reassuring noises through which the clang of the iron-shod boots on the cobbles broke ominously.

The boots ground to a halt, and three holes in the cover, brilliant diamond-points of light, went suddenly black. Couching, the cat waited, then sneezed and drew back as the tarpaulin was thrown up and glaring white sunlight struck at her eyes.

She stood over her kittens, the fur of her back bristling and the pupils of her eyes narrowed to pin-points. A kitten mewed plaintively.

For a moment, the hired man stared stupidly at his discovery, then turned towards the stable and called harshly: 'Hi, Maister! Here a wee.'

A second pair of boots clattered across the yard, and the face of the farmer, elderly, dark and taciturn, turned down on the cats.

'So that's whaur she's been,' commented the newcomer slowly.

He bent down to count the kittens and the cat struck at him, scoring a red furrow across the back of his wrist. He caught her by the neck and flung her roughly aside. Mewing she came back and began to lick her kittens. The Master turned away.

'Get rid of them,' he ordered. 'There's ower mony cats aboot this place.'

'Aye, Maister,' said the hired man.

Catching the mother he carried her, struggling and swearing, to the stable, flung her in, and latched the door. From the loft he secured an old potato sack and with this in his hand returned to the kittens.

There were five, and he noticed their tigerish markings without comprehending as, one by one, he caught them and thrust them into the bag. They were old enough to struggle, spitting, clawing and biting at his fingers.

Throwing the bag over his shoulder he stumped down the hill to the burn, stopping twice on the way to wipe the sweat that trickled down his face and neck, rising in beads between the roots of his lint-white hair.

Behind him, the buildings of the farm-steading shimmered in the heat. The few trees on the slope raised dry, brittle branches towards a sky bleached almost white. The smell of the farm, mingled with peat-reek, dung, cattle, milk, and the dark tang of the soil, was strong in his nostrils, and when he halted there was no sound but his own breathing and the liquid burbling of the burn.

Throwing the sack on the bank, he stepped into the stream. The water was low, and grasping a great boulder in the bed of the burn he strained to lift it, intending to make a pool.

He felt no reluctance at performing the execution. He had no feelings about the matter. He had drowned kittens before. He would drown them again.

Panting with his exertion, the hired man cupped water between his hands and dashed it over his face and neck in a glistening shower. Then he turned to the sack and its prisoners.

He was in time to catch the second kitten as it struggled out of the bag. Thrusting it back and twisting the mouth of the sack close, he went after the other. Hurrying on the sun-browned grass, treacherous as ice, he slipped and fell headlong, but grasped the runaway in his outflung hand.

It writhed round immediately and sank needle-sharp teeth into his thumb so that he grunted with pain and shook it from him. Unhurt, it fell by a clump of whins and took cover beneath them.

The hired man, his stolidity shaken by frustration tried to follow. The whins were thick and, scratched for his pains, he drew back, swearing flatly, without colour or passion.

Stooping, he could see the eyes of the kitten staring at him from the shadows under the whins. Its back was arched, its fur erect, its mouth open, and its thin lips drawn back over its tiny white teeth.

The hired man saw, again without understanding, the beginnings of tufts on the flattened ears. In his dull mind he felt a dark resentment at this creature which defied him. Rising, he passed his hand up his face in heavy thought, then slithering down to the stream, he began to gather stones. With an armful of small water-washed pebbles he returned to the whins.

First he strove to strike at the kitten from above. The roof of the whins was matted and resilient. The stones could not penetrate it. He flung straight then – to maim or kill – but the angle was difficult and only one missile reached its mark, rebounding from the ground and striking the kitten a glancing blow on the shoulder.

Kneeling, his last stone gone, the hired man watched, the red in his face deepening and thin threads of crimson rising in the whites of his eyes as the blood mounted to his head. A red glow of anger was spreading through his brain. His mouth worked and twisted to an ugly rent.

'Wait – wait,' he cried hoarsely, and, turning, ran heavily up the slope to the trees. He swung his whole weight on a low-hanging branch, snapping it off with a crack like a gun-shot.

Seated on the warm, short turf, the hired man prepared his weapon, paring at the end of the branch till the point was sharp as a dagger. When it was ready he knelt on his left knee and swung the branch to find the balance. The kitten was almost caught.

The savage lance-thrust would have skewered its body as a trout is spiked on the beak of a heron, but the point, slung too low, caught in a fibrous root and snapped off short. Impotently the man jabbed with his broken weapon while the kitten retreated disdainfully to the opposite fringe of the whins.

In the slow-moving mind of the hired man the need to destroy the kitten had become an obsession. Intent on this victim, he forgot the others abandoned by the burn side; forgot the passage of time, and the hard labour of the day behind him. The kitten, in his distorted mind, had grown to a monstrous thing, centring all the frustrations of a brutish existence. He craved to kill. . . .

But so far the honours lay with the antagonist.

In a sudden flash of fury the man made a second bodily assault on the whins and a second time retired defeated.

He sat down on the grass to consider the next move as the first breath of the breeze wandered up the hill. As though that were the signal, in the last moments of the sun, a lark rose, close at hand, and mounted the sky on the flood of its own melody.

The man drank in the coolness thankfully, and, taking a pipe from his pocket, lit the embers of tobacco in the bowl. He flung the match from him, still alight, and a dragon's tongue of amber flame ran over the dry grass before the breeze, reached a bare patch of sand and flickered out. Watching it, the hired man knitted his brows and remembered the heather-burning, and mountain hares that ran before the scarlet terror. And he looked at the whins.

The first match blew out in the freshening wind, but at the second the bush burst into crackling flame.

The whins were alight on the leeward side and burned slowly against the wind. Smoke rose thickly, and sparks and lighted shivers of wood sailed off on the wind to light new fires on the grass of the hillside.

Coughing as the pungent smoke entered his lungs, the man circled the clump till the fire was between him and the farm. He could see the kitten giving ground slowly before the flame. He thought for a moment of lighting this side of the clump also and trapping it between two fires; took his matches from his pocket, hesitated, and replaced them. He could wait.

Slowly, very slowly, the kitten backed towards him. The wind fought for it, delaying, almost holding the advance of the fire through the whins.

Showers of sparks leaped up from the bushes that crackled and spluttered as they burned, but louder than the crackling of the whins, from the farm on the slope of the hill, came another noise – the clamour of voices. The hired man walked clear of the smoke that obscured his view and stared up the hill.

The thatch of the farmhouse, dry as tinder, was aflare.

Gaping, he saw the flames spread to the roof of the byre, to the stables; saw the farmer running the horses to safety, and heard the thunder of hooves as the scared cattle, turned loose, rushed from the yard. He saw a roof collapse in an uprush of smoke and sparks, while a kitten, whose sire was a wild cat, passed out of the whins unnoticed and took refuge in a deserted burrow.

From there, with cold, defiant eyes, it regarded the hired man steadfastly.

TALKING POINTS

1. The first sequence of this story, up to the point where the cat is separated from the kittens and thrown into the stable, is told from the viewpoint of the cat. Pick out and comment on some of the details that build up this impression of the cat's world; and consider the effect of the sparing use of dialogue in this part.
2. The middle part of the story is presented from the point of view of the hired man struggling with the kittens. Indicate the main stages of the conflict between the man and the escaping kitten; and consider, if you like, the effect of the setting on the man's consciousness and the progress of the story.
3. The hired man is never given a name. What do you think is gained by this anonymity?
4. Read the conclusion again (the last paragraph), and discuss its significance for the whole story. Add, if you like, a comment on the shaping and design of the story generally.
5. What do you make of the burning of the house in the context of the human action in the story?

Fred Urquhart (b. 1912)

THE BIKE

The bicycle cost her seven pounds ten. It took her almost three years to save the amount. She did without the pictures and new stockings and sweets and lots of other things to get it. The other girls in the wash-house laughed at her determination to save. When they sent Tammy for pies and ice-cream and lemonade they always tried to coax her to get some, too. And they laughed at her refusals and said she was mean. They could not understand her desire to have a bike.

'What dae ye want a bike for, onyway?' Lizzie the forewoman said. 'What guid's it goin' to dae ye?'

'I don't know,' Annie said. 'I just want a bike.'

She could not put into words her longing to sail along superbly, skimming like a yacht in full sail. The only argument she could find in its favour was that it would save car fares. 'It costs me fourpence a day to get here,' she said. 'I'd save that if I cycled. Five fourpences and twopence on Saturdays. What's that?'

'Guidness knows,' Lizzie said. 'I never was ony guid at coontin'.'

'Twenty-two pennies,' Annie said, her brows wrinkled with the effort of calculation. 'That's one and – one and tenpence.'

'Ay, it's a guid bit oot o' ten bob a week,' Lizzie said.

'Well, it's time we got on! Harry's yellin' aboot thae Domingo Souza bottles no' bein' labelled yet.'

Still, although the other girls in the wine and spirit merchant's warehouse saw that Annie's reasons for wanting a bicycle were good, it did not prevent them from jeering at her for saving. They said she was a mug not to get it on the instalment system. Annie refused to do that, however. It was too much like getting a thing 'on tick'. And so she saved and dreamed. Dreamed of the time when she would be able to dash along freely without feeling crushed on the crowded pavements.

But the three years were long when she saw the number of pies the other girls consumed and the bottles of lemonade they tilted to their dry mouths. Sometimes she thought it wasn't worth it: the bike seemed as far away as ever. And she would look at the little penny-bank-book that was all that she had to show for her scrimping, and she thought often of blowing the whole amount on a new coat or on a trip to Blackpool. But she sternly set her mind against the temptations that the other girls whispered to her. And at last she got her bike.

It was a lovely bike. A low racer, painted a bright red, with cold gleaming chromium-plated handle-bars. The first morning she passed her hand proudly over its shining mudguards before she jumped upon it and whisked along to her work. She wouldn't need to steal any more rides on her brother's bike! Here was something of her own: something she could clean and oil and tend; something she could keep shining and spruce. Her heart sang with exhilaration and proud accomplishment, keeping time with her feet working the pedals and the wheels going round. She had a bike! *Oh, Georgia's got a moon, and I have got a bike! The one I've waited for, and I have got a bike!* And she waved gaily as she passed Lizzie and Meg and Bessie walking to the warehouse.

She put the bike behind the barrels at the back of the washhouse. It was safely out of the way there.

Everybody in the warehouse came to admire it. 'It's a nice wee bike,' said one of the lorry-drivers. 'Ye look real smart on it. I saw ye wheech past the tram-car I was on this morning, and I said to masel' "Is that Annie?" Ay, ye're a real smarter!'

'What did ye say ye paid for it?' asked Charlie, the youngest lorry-driver.

'Seven pounds ten,' Annie said shyly.

'Oh boy!' Charlie whistled with astonishment. 'Some capitalist made a pile out o' that. Ye were a mug to encourage him. Fools and their money!'

Charlie was always talking about the capitalists and about wage-slaves and socialism and the revolution. He was a loud-voiced, swaggering young man, rather good-looking in a flashy sort of way. Although he was never properly shaved and always wore a muffler instead of a collar and tie, Annie was very much attracted by him. But he never encouraged her either by look or by word, and she was too shy to show that she liked him.

That afternoon as Annie returned to work she overtook Charlie at the gate of the warehouse. She jumped off her bike and walked with him towards the wash-house.

'Ay, it's a nice bike,' he said, eyeing it critically. 'How much did ye say ye paid for it again?'

'Seven pounds ten.'

Charlie whistled tunelessly. He slouched along with his hands in his pockets. At the door of the wash-house he made no move to leave her. He leaned against the door-post. Annie stood, holding the bike, watching him, admiring the yellow curls that dangled over his low brown forehead.

'Seen that picter at the Gaiety?' Charlie said.

Annie shook her head. She caressed the bike's leather seat.

'Like to see it?'

'I was goin' tonight,' she said.

'Yourself?'

'Uhuh.'

'Mind if I chum you?'

'Okay,' she said.

All afternoon Annie could hardly work for thinking about going to the pictures with Charlie. Even the bike was overshadowed by this wonderful happening. She could hardly take her tea for thinking of what lay ahead, and she was at the corner of Commercial Street ten minutes before the time.

She hardly recognized Charlie when he mooched up to her with his hands in his pockets. He was wearing a collar and tie and a scarlet pullover, and his bright yellow hair was neatly arranged into waves like corrugated iron. It looked as though it had just been marcelled.

'Oke,' he said, balancing himself on his sharp-pointed shoes on the edge of the pavement.

Annie smiled. She pranced along proudly at his side in the direction of the Gaiety. She tried to think of something to say, but she could think of nothing. Charlie kept his eyes on the pavement, a cigarette dangling from his lips.

At the pay-box Annie fumbled in her bag. 'It's okay,' Charlie said, 'I'll get it again.' And he bent down to the bowl and said: 'Two sixpennies.'

The Pathé Gazette was showing. Annie was not much interested in soldiers marching and in naval reviews. She looked sideways at Charlie. He was slumped down in his seat, his hands in his pockets. Annie admired his profile in the semi-darkness.

The feature film started. It was a torrid romance. Annie placed her hand on her knee close to Charlie's leg. He made no response for a long time. Annie could not enjoy the film for wondering why not. Then about the end of the film Charlie placed his hand over hers. But he took it away when the lights went up.

They said nothing as they walked to Annie's house. She slipped her hand through his arm, but he never took his hands out of his pockets.

'Well, I'll see you tomorrow,' he said at the door of the tenement. 'Cheerio!'

'Cheerio!' Annie said.

At first Annie kept the bike in the wash-house, but the foreman advised her to keep it elsewhere. 'Ye'd better watch it doesnie get scratched here, lass,' he said. 'If I was you, I'd put it in the garage. It would be safer there.'

But Annie discovered that the bike was not as safe in the garage as it had been in the wash-house under her own eye. The boys in the office and the two louts who looked after the yard were always racing it around the yard. She began to notice marks on the paint, and sometimes when she went to get it she found that the seat had been raised.

'If I was you, I'd tell thae galoots where they got off,' Lizzie said. 'Especially that lazy brute, James. It would be wicer-like if he helped puir Tammy to sweep up the yard instead o' racin' roond and roond.'

But James did not heed Lizzie when she gave him a flyting. 'Awa' and mind yer ain business,' he said.

And he continued to cycle madly around the yard whenever Harry, the foreman, was out of the way, leaving Tammy, a simple-looking youth of about seventeen, to do all the work.

Annie would have brought the bike back into the wash-house, but they got in an extra lot of barrels and there was no room for it. Sometimes she thought that she would be better to leave the bike at home and take the tram to work as she used to do. But although she was now getting twelve and sixpence a week she could not afford anything from it for tram fares. She went to the pictures once a week with Charlie and she always paid herself. Lately, too, they had taken to going to dances, which meant spending one and sixpence or two shillings which she could ill afford.

Apart from her dislike of James for using her bike, she disliked him for his influence on Charlie. They were as thick as thieves. Every night after work they went into the public house at the end of the street, although already they had drunk all the wine and whisky they could scrounge from the warehouse. 'I'd like to see their insides,' Lizzie said. 'They'll be bonnie and burned!'

Whenever Charlie had too much drink he talked about 'the capitalists grinding the faces of the poor', and there were always several adjectives describing the capitalists. But he had so great a capacity for drink that it was difficult to tell when he had had too much. Annie hated to see him at those times, though she was fascinated and could not help listening to what he was saying. She was terrified that he would drink too much at the dances they went to and cause her to feel embarrassed.

One forenoon six or seven weeks after Annie had bought the bicycle, Charlie was in such a state that even the foreman remarked upon it. 'He's awa' oot as fu' as a puggy,' he said to Lizzie. 'And him wi' a load o' stuff on his lorry that's worth thoosands. I hope he's able to deliver it a', and that nothin' happens to him.'

But Charlie was able to deliver all his orders safely at the various pubs and licensed grocers. He returned to the ware-house about five o'clock, and his lorry swung into the yard far too quickly for the amount of space available.

'That yin'll kill somebody yin o' thae days, if he's no' carefu',' said Lizzie, looking out of the wash-house.

'He's needin' taken doon a peg,' Bessie said, wiping her red hands on her packsheet apron and scowling over Lizzie's shoulder at the boastful Charlie as he swung empty boxes and crates from his lorry on to the ground. 'I havenie forgotten aboot what he did to the puir cat.'

This had happened some time before. The cat was a great favourite with everybody in the warehouse except Charlie. It was a good ratter, and when it was about, the girls weren't afraid to plunge their hands into the straw in the crates: they knew there was no danger of rats lurking there when Towser was about.

But one day Charlie had swung his lorry into the yard and headed straight for the cat, which was lying stretched out in the sun. Somebody had noticed and cried a warning. But

Charlie had taken no notice, and the wheels had gone right over the animal. And when Lizzie and Bessie had lashed him furiously with their tongues, Charlie had laughed and said: 'The beast had no right to be lying there.'

'He'll get an awfu' drop yin o' thae days,' Bessie muttered now. 'I only hope I'm there when he gets it.'

'Me too,' said Meg.

'Lookit the way he's chuckin' the boxes doon and leavin' them lyin' for puir Tammy to put in their places,' Lizzie said.

'That's a socialist for ye,' Bessie said.

'Thae kind that talk sae big aboot their socialism are aye the worst,' Lizzie said.

Annie felt that she should champion Charlie, but she could think of nothing to say. She continued to wind pink tissue wrappers around bottles of Lodestar Ruby Wine.

Having thrown off every box and crate, Charlie jumped into the driving-seat and started his lorry. He headed straight for the garage door. 'He'll run into it if he doesnie look oot', Lizzie said.

But he managed to scrape through. 'That was a near thing,' Lizzie said, turning and picking up a crate of empty bottles.

Just then there was a crash. It was not very loud, but it was loud enough for the sound to be unfamiliar. 'What's that?' Bessie cried.

The four girls ran into the yard. Harry had already run out of the office, and some of the young clerks were following him. They approached the garage door.

Charlie met them. He was grinning broadly. 'It's okay,' he said.

'What was that noise?' Harry said.

'That!' Charlie shrugged. 'That was just that lassie's bike. What did she need to leave it for in the middle o' the garage?'

Numbly Annie stared at the twisted wheels and the broken red frame. She scarcely heard the arguments that went on around her. Dimly she heard Lizzie shriek: 'That's that James goin' and leavin' it lyin' there in the middle o' the floor!' And even more dimly she heard Charlie reply: 'Dy'e think I'm lookin' oot for every heap o' scrap-iron that's in my way?'

That night Annie cried herself to sleep. Harry had assured her that she would get a new bike. 'I'll make Charlie and James pay it between them,' he promised her. 'Charlie can rant as much as he likes about the insurance being liable, but I'll see that he pays for it.'

But Annie knew that even if she got another bike it would never be the same. She would always remember Charlie's derisive grin as he looked down at the broken frame, and his scornful words. She knew that something more than her bike had been broken. Nothing would ever be the same again.

TALKING POINTS

1. The first part of the story deals with the first theme – Annie's desire to buy the bike. Discuss the difficulties and temptations that she had to face; account for her determination and success; and comment on the language used to describe her feelings when she acquires the bike.
2. The second part of the story deals with the second theme: it could be called 'Annie and Charlie'. Indicate how this part is linked to the first, and describe the aspects of Charlie's character that are shown up here.
3. The third part concentrates on Charlie and his destructive tendencies. Describe briefly the two main events that result from these tendencies and the reactions of the other workers to Charlie's behaviour.
4. 'She knew that something more than her bike had been broken.' Discuss the effect achieved by the author at the end of the story in drawing the two main themes together. What impression are we left with?
5. 'Nothing would ever be the same again.' With this as a theme, discuss Annie's experiences in the story.
6. In what ways does Annie's relationship with Charlie resemble her relationship with the bike?

George Mackay Brown (b. 1921)

A TREADING OF GRAPES

The parish church of St Peter's stands at one end of a sandy
bay on the west coast of Orkney. It is a small square stone
utilitarian structure built in the year 1826 by the freely-given
labour of all the parishioners; women are said to have carried
the stones from the quarry three miles away on their backs, a
slow, holy, winter-long procession. But there were churches
there before the present church was erected. The inscribed
tombs in the churchyard go back to the seventeenth century,
and there are older anonymous stones. The minister of St
Peter's in the year 1795 was the Rev. Dr Thomas Fortheringhame. He was the author of two volumes of sermons published
in Edinburgh. He complained in a written account of the
parish that 'the Kirk roof is full of leakings and dribblings in
the winter time, and of draughts at all seasons of the year,
whereby the parishioners are like to catch their death of cold,
and often my discourses are broken by reason of their hoast-
ings and coughings. The masonry is much dilapidated. . . .'
It was soon after this that plans were drawn up by the laird
for the building of the present church on the same site. But
there were other churches there even before Dr Fortheringhame's wet and draughty edifice. Among the clustering tombstones is a piece of a wall with a weathered hole in it that
looks as though it might have been an arched window, and
slightly to one side an abrupt squat arrangement of dressed
stones that suggests an altar. The Rev. Dr Fortheringhame
says curtly, 'There is in the vicinity of the Kirk remnants of a
popish chapel, where the ignorant yet resort in time of sick-

ness and dearth to leave offerings, in the vain hope that such superstition will alleviate their sufferings; the which Romish embers I have exerted myself to stamp out with all severity during the period of my ministry. . . .' Of this older church nothing is known, except that the priest here at the time of the Reformation was called Master John Halcrow. A fragment of a sermon – for the second Sunday after Epiphany in the year 1548 – was recently discovered in a folder of old documents in the laird's cellar. Script and parchment are in the style of the early sixteenth century, and it is possible that Father Halcrow was the preacher.

The source of Father Halcrow's sermon is the gospel account of the wedding feast at Cana in Galilee. Since we also have sermons on the same text by Dr Fortheringhame (August 1788) and by the present incumbent, Rev. Garry Watters, B.D. (Edin.) – the latter sermon preached earlier this year and reproduced by courtesy of the editor of the parish magazine – it might be of interest, as showing the changing style of the Scottish sermon through the centuries, to set them out, one after the other, beginning with that of Mr Watters.

*   *   *

(1)

REV. GARRY WATTERS

'I wonder what you were thinking of, when you listened to this New Testament lesson? I'm sure some of you were thinking of the last wedding you were at, perhaps a month ago, or a year ago, or even ten years ago. You were thinking, of course, of the church, and the young couple standing there together in the empty choir, and the minister in solemn tones performing the marriage ceremony. Yes, but I suppose that you were thinking particularly of the reception afterwards in the hotel, for this piece of scripture, strangely enough, has nothing to say about the marriage ceremony at all; it's all about the reception. I'm sure you're seeing again in your mind's eye all the cars standing in the hotel car park, and the long tables covered with flowers and food, and guests being introduced to one another, and then – a crowning moment – when the happy young couple entered to take their places, with confetti in the bride's veil and on the shoulders of the bridegroom's new suit. Then the meal, to the accompaniment of lighthearted conversation, and the toasts and the speeches – some wittier than others, I suppose – and the reading of the many telegrams, and the furtive moment when the young newly-weds slip away to their secret honeymoon destination. Perhaps there will have been a talented singer or two among the guests. Certainly there was music and dancing. This never-to-be-forgotten day ended with the singing of Auld Lang Syne.

'Yes, you remember it all vividly. What you will have forgotten, in the sheer enjoyment of it all, is how smoothly everything happened. Everything went to schedule. But – and now I'm coming to the important thing – you would certainly have remembered this wedding, with some pain and embarrassment, if, for example, the organist had played Wagner instead of Mendelssohn for the entry of the bride, or if the wedding cake had not been delivered from the baker's in time, or if the toast order had got all mixed up, or if the taximen had driven the bride's parents to the wrong hotel.

'Now this is exactly what happened in the gospel story – somebody blundered. The refreshments ran done. The whole wedding reception was threatened with disaster. A thing like that is remembered for a long time in a small place. In the little town of Cana they would have gossiped about this badly-organized wedding for many a day, would they not?

'Fortunately, Jesus was a guest at the wedding, and he very

quickly put things to right, at once, no nonsense about it; smoothly and efficiently he took over, and everything was straightened out. Not only that, but the wedding went with a greater swing than before.

'We read about miracles, but – ask yourselves this – what exactly is a miracle? It is not some kind of superior conjuring trick – it is rather, I'm inclined to think myself, the exercise of a supreme common sense, a looking at every conceivable eventuality with absolute clear-sightedness and understanding, so that the remedy is clear even before the difficulty arises. Turning water into wine is merely a graphic shorthand for the way in which the foresight of Jesus more than compensated for the steward's blundering. He made sure beforehand that the neglected supplies were to hand.

'He is the best organizer, the best planner who ever lived. You may be sure we can trust him with our smallest everyday affairs. He won't ever let us down.

'Think, in the wider sphere, what a brilliant business executive, what a wise ambassador, what a competent minister of state he would have made! In his hands we can safely leave the troubles and frictions that distract the world we live in. Amen.

'There's just one thing I must mention before the final hymn. Up to now, in this church, on the four occasions each year that we celebrate the Sacrament of the Lord's Supper, a wine has been used that contained a certain small percentage of alcohol. Of recent years there has been, in this congregation and indeed all over Scotland, a large and growing demand for unfermented wine to be used in the sacrament, as being more seemly. Consequently, next Sunday, after the morning service, a ballot will be taken of all the members of the congregation present, as to whether you want fermented wine at future sacraments, or an unfermented substitute more in keeping, it may be, with the seemliness of our devotions.'

(2)

Dr Thomas Fortheringhame

'Brethren, some of you might be thinking that the piece of gospel I read out just this minute anent the Lord Christ's turning of water into wine at Cana of Galilee is divine permission to you to make drunken beasts of yourselves at every wedding that takes place within the bounds of this parish this coming winter; ay, and not only at every wedding but at every christening forby and every funeral and harvest supper. It is the devil of hell that has put such a thought into your minds. It never says in holy writ that any wedding guest was drunk at Cana of Galilee.

'Magnus Learmonth, you in the second pew from the back, at the wedding you made for your third lass Deborah at Skolness at the back end of Lammas, all the guests lay at the ale-kirn like piglets about the teats of a sow till morning, to the neglect even of dancing; and two women in this same district came to themselves next morning in the ditch of Graygyres. Bella Simison, you do well to hang your head there at the back of the Kirk – it argues a small peck of grace. Andrina of Breck, you were the other defaulter – don't look at me like that, woman! – you have a brazen outstaring impudence commensurate with your debauchery. Well I know you and your runnings back and fore between Breck and the ale-house with your bit flask under your shawl. Things are told privily into my lug.

'What this text argues, brethren, is that the host at the wedding, the bridegroom's good-father, was a careful and a prudent man with his bawbees. No doubt this provident man said to himself the day the marriage bids were sent about the countryside with a hired horseman, "If I order too few pigs of drink, they'll say I keep the purse-strings drawn over tight, and if I order too muckle they'll say I'm a spendthrift. And so

I find myself between devil and deep. What is the right quantity of drink for a celebration such as this?" . . . Being a prudent man, I say, he ordered too few pigs of drink (only it wasn't pigs of usquebaugh, whisky, in that foreign place, nor yet ale; it was jars of wine). The which when the Lord came he corrected, he set to right, as he will beyond a doubt set to right all our exaggerations and our deficiencies, since only he kens what is stinted and what is overblown in the nature of every man born. He adds and he takes from. The stringent economy of the host drew no rebuke from him. He accomplished the miracle. Then there was dancing, then there was fiddling, then no doubt near midnight bride and groom were carried into the ben room with roughness and sly jokes and a fiddle and five lanterns.

'Nor was this the end of meat and drink as far as the Lord was concerned. You ken all about the multiplication of the five bannocks and the two cod-fish, concerning which I preached to you for an hour and more last Sabbath. There came a night at the supper-board when he suddenly took an oat-cake and broke it and raised his jug of drink and leaned across and said to them who were no doubt wanting to fill their bellies without any palaver, "This is my body," he said, and then, "This is my blood" – a most strange and mystifying comparison indeed, that the papists would have us believe to be a literal and real and wholly breath-taking change of substance effected by a form of words. Whatever it means, brethren – and our General Assembly has not and doubtless will not bind you to any infallible conclusions as to the significance of these utterances – whatever it means, it teaches us a terrible reverence for the things we put in our mouths to nourish us, whether it is the laird's grouse and claret or the limpets that Sam of the Shore eats with cold water out of the well in the lean days of March.

'You will not go home, therefore, and hog down your brose like swine in a sty or like cuddies at a trough. The common things you put in your mouths are holy mysteries indeed, beyond the taste and the texture. Therefore, brethren, with reverence you will make them a part of your body and your life.

'Prudence, my brethren, a proper proportioning of our goods, estimation, forethought – so much to the King, so much to the laird, so much to the Kirk, so much for the maintainance of ourselves and them that belong to us, so much to the poor – that is doubtless the meaning of this text; and for the things we lack, that we should ask the Lord to supply them, and so rest content in our estate.

'John Sweynson, I observe that you bought a new shawl to your wife's head at the Kirkwall Market, with what looks to be silken lacing round the edge of it, a thing of vanity, and new black lace gloves to her hands. She will not darken this kirk door again, no nor you either, with these Babylonish things on her body.

'Samuel Firth, of the operations of your farm, Dale in the district of Kirkbister, naturally I ken nothing, nor does it concern me. But you have seven black cows on the hill if you have one, and fifty sheep forby, and a hundred geese. Is it a proper and a godly thing, think you, that your three small bairns sit in the front pew there under the precentor blue and channering with the cold, they having no right sarks to their backs nor boots to their feet? Have a care of this, look to it, as you call yourself a Christian. Amen.

'Concluding, I have two announcements to make. John Omand, on account of the bastard child he fathered on Maria Riddoch at Michelmas, appeared before the Kirk session on Wednesday and being duly constrained answered *Yea* to the accusation, wherefore he will suffer public rebuke three sequent Sabbaths in this Kirk on the stool of penitence, beginning next Sabbath.

'I hear that the French brig *Merle*, Monsieur Claude Devereux, master, discharged some cargo at the Bay of Ostray in the darkness of Friday night. The gentlemen of the excise were at Kirkwall, playing at cartes. Will you, therefore, James Drever, deliver as usual a keg of best brandy at the Manse tomorrow morning, when Mistress Skea my serving woman will see that you are recompensed for your pains.'

(3)

FATHER HALCROW

The Vine: 'Cometh the full grape cluster upon the vine. The rain falleth. Clusters thicken, purple they are as bruises, as thunder, yet each grape containeth within itself a measure of joy and dancing, the quick merry blood of the earth.

Grape Harvest: 'Cometh at last the hour of full ripeness. Labourers toil all day, they cram the baskets, their arms are red. The master of the vineyard, he goeth about the streets in the last of the sun, bargaining with such as sit idle against the wall and them that throw dice in the dust. For the grape harvest must be ingathered.

The Treading of Grapes: 'And he that presseth the hoarded grapes, look, his breast and his thighs are red, as though he had endured a terrible battle, himself scatheless. And still more and more grapes are brought to the press where he laboureth, this hero.

Wine: 'Now it standeth long, the vat, in a cellar under earth, as it were in a cold grave. Yet this is in no wise a station of death. Put thy ear against the vat, thou hearest a ceaseless murmur, a slow full suspiration. The juice is clothing itself in sound, in song, in psalmody.

The Wine Shop: 'Now see the vinter in his shop, bottles, barrels, wineskins all about him. There cometh a steward that

is preparing a wedding, a feast of note, his master's daughter
will be married. This feast is not to be any mouse-in-the-
cupboard affair, no, it will be a costly ceremony with harps
and tapestries and bits of silver thrown to the children in the
street outside. What does the vinter think – will seven jars of
wine be enough? Or twelve? Or three? It is hard to say how
much the guests will drink. Many strangers are bidden. They
might sip with small burgess mouths or they might have
throats like salt mines. He cannot tell.

The Six Jars: 'In the end they agreed together upon so many
jars of wine, six let us say, after much calculation according
to the wisdom of this world.

The Guests: 'Under the first star they travel, the wedding
guests, such a crowd as you would see on any Orkney feast
day – ploughman and mason and laird and labourer and
grieve and notary and beachcomber, and a horde of women,
besides one or two persons unbidden – in holy-day coats they
crowd to one house with lights and music in it. There they
will celebrate the sacrificial feast of a maidenhead.

The Word: 'And presently in the door stands the carpenter of
Nazareth, and his mother and twelve more forby that have a
smell of fish and seaweed and limpets on them from their
trade, all known faces. Yet none guessed that here was The
Incarnate Word (had they not bargained with him for cradles
and chairs and roof-beams?). None knew that here was Mary,
Queen of Angels, Mystical Rose, Gate of Heaven, Holy
Mother of God (had she not washed her linen a many a time
with the other women at the burn?).

Rose of Love: 'A bell strikes silence upon their babble. From
this door and that door bridegroom and bride issue, separately
they come forth. They stand together at last. They wait for
all their random lusts, longings, desires, burnings to be
gathered up into the one rose of human love. Cometh a

priest and blesseth them. Then all the harps break out in one concert of joy.

The Empty Jars: 'The steward maketh a sign. Now is the time for all those guests – rich and poor, young and old, farmer and fisherman, widow and maiden, to mingle together – so that this chamber seemeth to be in little the whole world and its tumultuous folk. The first jar is emptied into a hundred cups. The bridegroom, where is he? Secretly twelve hand-maidens light lamps. The bridegroom has gone into his chamber. The handmaidens carry the bride through a door. The harps play. The steward is busy between the music and the wine. The cups go round and round. A handful of silver sklinters like rain among the children in the dark close outside. Sand runs in the hourglass, candles dwindle, the night passeth. And then one cometh, a serving man, and saith to the steward *The wine is all finished* while as yet the first flush is not upon the faces of musicians and dancers.

The Water: 'Consider what a common thing is water. We set small value upon it except when the well is nothing but a few burning stones. When there is abundance of water we turn up the collars of our coats and we curse the rain. I tell you the guests at that marriage feast in Cana thought but poorly of it when the empty wine jars were filled to the brim with water at the behest of this carpenter from Nazareth. And the steward was distraught and the host's brow dark with vexation; he was like to be held in disgrace a many a day for his improvidence. And yet the woman reassureth the entire company, *Quodcumque dixerit vobis, facite* – "Do whatsoever he telleth you to do." So sweetly she urgeth that the serving men run to obey. Now the as-yet-unmiracled Word standeth among the water jars.

The Miracle: 'The souls and creatures of that house – in particular the element of water – become utterly subject unto The Word, as all creation was in the six days of its becoming. The devious stations by which water becometh wine – the tap-root, grafting, pruning, sun, blossoming, wind, fruition, harvest, press, leaven, vat, vintry – all that long vexation was here cancelled. The Word spanned all creation, as it did in the paradise of Eden before Adam delved and Eve span. And a serving man poureth a jar of this new water. At once their cups brim with red circles. The trembling lips of the steward approve the mystery. Then all their mouths break out in celebration, like angels and holy souls that praise God forever with their *Sanctus* and their *Gloria*.

* * *

'Dear children, this I have spoken of is a most famous marriage. We are poor people, fishermen, and crofters, and we think it is not likely in these the days of our vanity that we will be bidden to such a feast. We are poor people, Olaf the fisherman and Jock the crofter and Merran the hen-wife, we are pleased enough with oatcakes and ale at our weddings, we were born to hunger and meikle hardship, and there will be a single candle burning beside us the night they come to straik us and to shroud us.

'No, but this is not true. Let me tell you a secret. Christ the King, he hath uplifted our fallen nature as miraculously as he clothed water in the red merry robes of wine. Very rich and powerful you are, princes, potentates, heirs and viceroys of a Kingdom. So opulent and puissant are you, dear ones, for that each one of you has in his keeping an immortal soul, a rich jewel indeed, more precious than all the world beside. So then, princes (for I will call you Olaf the fisherman and Jock the crofter no longer but I will call you by the name the Creator will call you in the last day) princes, I say, I have good news for you, you are bidden every one to a wedding. Get ready your gifts, get ready your shoes to the journey. *What wedding?* you ask, *we know of no wedding*. I answer, *The marriage of Christ with His Church. And where will this marriage be?* you ask. *Everywhere,* I answer, *but in particular, lords and princes, in this small kirk beside the sea where you sit. And when is it to be, this wedding?* you ask me. *Always,* I answer, *but in particular within this hour, now, at the very moment when I bow over this bread of your offering, the food, princes and lords, that you have won with such hard toil from the furrows, at once when I utter upon it five words* HIC EST ENIM CORPUS MEUM. Then is Christ the King come once again to his people, as truly as he was present at the marriage in Cana, and the Church his bride abides his coming, and this altar with the few hosts on it and the cup is a rich repast indeed, a mingling of the treasures of earth and heaven, and the joy of them in Cana is nothing to the continual merriment of the children of God. *Sanctus sanctus sanctus,* they cry for ever and ever, *Benedictus qui venit in nomine Domini.*

'Dance ye then, princes and ladies, in your homespun, there is no end to this marriage, it goes on at every altar of the world, world without end. This Bread that I will raise above your kneeling, It is entire Christ – Annunciation, Nativity, Transfiguration, Passion, Death, Resurrection, Ascension, Majesty, gathered up into one perfect offering, the Divine Love itself, whereof you are witnesses.

'And not only you, princes, all creation rejoices in the marriage of Christ and His Church, animals, fish, plants, yea, the water, the wind, the earth, the fire, stars, the very smallest grains of dust that blow about your cornfields and your Kirkyards.'

In Nomine Patris et Filii et Spiritus Sancti. Amen.

*   *   *

I walked along the road past St Peter's church this morning. On the beach a few fishing boats were hauled out of reach of the waves. Behind the church lay the farms and crofts of the parish, tilth and pasture, the mill, the school, the smithy, the shop. In the field next the church a tractor moved jerkily, trailing an airy drove of gulls; it is the time of ploughing. The young man in the tractor seat suddenly stood up and shouted, he swung his arm in wide circles. A girl throwing oats to a white agitation of hens at the end of a byre two fields away acknowledged his summons with a mere movement of her hand, a suggestion of greeting. Then she went quickly indoors (so that the neighbours wouldn't be getting any ideas for gossip). But the January air, I thought, was sweeter for that small promise of replenishment; and perhaps Mr Watters will soon have another wedding sermon to preach.

The sea shattered and shattered on the beach.

The wind from the sea soughed under the eaves of the Kirk, and among tombstones with texts and names newly chiselled on them, and those with withered half-obliterated lettering, and those that have lost their meanings and secrets to very ancient rain.

TALKING POINTS

1. The story is in the form of a triptych: three styles of preaching and three religious personalities are presented side by side and unified by the common text from John II. Describe and discuss these three contrasting styles and personalities, and the varying interpretations of the texts.
2. The story may be said to have a prologue and an epilogue. Discuss the advantages or effects gained by framing the three sermons between the author's personal description and comments.
3. Is there any religious or other significance in beginning with the contemporary sermon and moving backwards in time?
4. What linguistic devices or turns of phrase suggest the historical periods to which the sermons appear to belong?
5. By examining the style and form of each sermon, try to work out the author's own attitude to the three preachers, his own religious opinions and preferences.
6. What implied commentary on human life do the last two sentences make?

Iain Crichton Smith (b. 1928)

HOME

The black polished car drew up outside the brown tenement and he rested for a moment, his hands still on the wheel. He was a big man with a weatherbeaten red-veined face and a strong jaw. On one finger of his right hand was a square red ring. He looked both competent and hard.

After a while he got out, looking round him and up at the sky with a hungry look as if he were scanning the veldt. His wife in furs got out more slowly. Her face had a haggard brownness like that of a desiccated gipsy and seemed to be held together, like a lacy bag, by the wrinkles.

He looked up at the tenement with the cheerful animation of one who had left it, and yet with a certain curiosity.

'Lock the car, dear,' said his wife.

He looked at her for a moment in surprise and then said as if he had been listening to a witticism,

'But they don't steal things here.'

She smiled disdainfully.

They walked into the close whose walls were brown above and a dirty blue below, pitted with scars. Somebody had written in chalk the words YA BASS. It looked for a moment African, and he stared at it as if it had recalled some memory.

On the other side of the road the flat-faced shops looked back at them blankly.

He pointed upwards to a window.

'Do you mind the Jamiesons?' he said.

She remembered but took no pleasure in the memory.

The Jamiesons had lived above them and were, of course,

Protestant. Not that at that level you could distinguish Catholic from Protestant except that the former went to chapel and the latter didn't go anywhere. The O'Rahilly's house – for instance – had been full of wee ornaments, and once she had seen a complete ornamental house showing, outside it, like Europeans outside a veranda, Christ and the twelve disciples, the whole thing painted a distasteful green.

She remembered Jamieson all right. Every Friday night he would dress up in his best blue suit, neat as a ray or razor, and would wave to his wife who was following his progress to the road from an open window, her scarf tight round her head. He would go off to the pub and pick a fight with a Catholic, or more likely three Catholics. At midnight he would come home covered with blood, his face bruised a fine Protestant blue, his clothes dirty and brown. He would walk like a victorious gladiator up the stair and then start a fight with his wife, uprooting chairs and wardrobes till the silence of exhaustion settled over the flats at about one in the morning. The next day his wife would descend the stair, her eyes black and blue, and say that she had stumbled at the sink. Her repertoire of invention was endless.

'I remember,' she said.

The town had changed a lot since they had left it, that much was clear. Now the old tenements were being knocked down and the people shuttled out to huge featureless estates where the windows revealed the blue sky of TV. There were hardly any picture houses left: they had been converted into bingo halls. Instead of small shops supermarkets were springing up, flexing their huge muscles. The lover's lane had disappeared. The park seemed to have lost its atmosphere of pastoral carelessness and was being decorated for the visitors with literate slogans in flowers.

'It's thirty-five years since we left,' said her husband.

And the wallet bulged from his breast pocket, a wife, two children, and a good job in administration.

He moved about restlessly. He wanted to tell someone how well he had done but how could he do that? All the people he had known were gone elsewhere, many of them presumably dead and completely forgotten.

'Do you mind old Hannah?' he said.

She had been a fat old woman who sat day after day at the window leaning out of it talking to the passers-by. A fat woman with arthritis. He wondered vaguely what had happened to her.

'I wonder if the coal-house is still here. Come on.'

He took his wife by the hand and they walked down the close to the back. The coal-houses were incredibly still there, all padlocked and all beside each other, all with discoloured doors.

She kept her fur coat as far away from them as she could.

'Do you mind the day I went to the factor?' he said. The factor had been a small, buttoned-up, black-suited lawyer. In those days of poverty he himself had been frightened to visit him in his wee office with the dim glass door. He imagined what he would do to that factor now.

He had gone there after coming home from the office, and the wee lawyer in the undertaker's suit had said to him over his shoulder.

'What do you want?'

'I want to report the rain coming through the roof.'

'How much do you pay Jackson?'

'Fifteen shillings a week.'

'And what do you expect for fifteen shillings a week?' said the factor, as if even giving words away were an agony of the spirit. In a corner of the office an umbrella dripped what seemed to be black rain.

'I was hoping that the house would be dry anyway.'

'I'll send someone round tomorrow,' and the factor had bent down to study a ledger with a rusty red cover.

'You said that a week ago.'

'And I'm saying it again. I'm a busy man. I've got a lot to do.' At that moment he had been filled with a terrible reckless anger and was about to raise his fist when the factor looked up. His mouth opened slightly showing one gold tooth in the middle of the bottom row of teeth, and he said carefully,

'Next week.'

So he had walked out past the dispirited receptionist in the glass cage – the one with the limp and the ageing mother – and then home.

Thinking back on it now, he thought: I was treated like a black. That's what it amounted to. By God, like a black.

He wished that the factor was alive now so that he could show him his bank balance. The wee nyaff. The Scottish words rose unbidden to his mouth like bile.

For a moment he did in fact see himself as a black, cringing in that rotting office, suffering the contempt, hearing the black rain dripping behind him from the furled umbrella.

But then a black would buy a bicycle and forget all about his humiliation. Blacks weren't like us.

As he turned away from the coal-house door he saw the washing hanging from the ropes on the green.

'Ye widna like to be daeing that noo,' he told his wife jocularly.

'What would the Bruces say if they saw you running about in this dirty place like a schoolboy?' she said coldly.

'What dae ye mean?'

'Simply what I said. There was no need to come here at all. Or do you want to take a photograph and show it to them? "The Place Where I Was Born".'

'I wasna born here. I just lived here for five years.'

'What would they think of you, I wonder.'

'I don't give a damn about the Bruces,' he burst out, the veins on his forehead swelling. 'What's he but a doctor anyway? I'm not ashamed of it. And, by God, why should you be ashamed of it? You weren't brought up in a fine house either. You worked in a factory till I picked you up at that dance.'

She turned away.

'Do you mind that night?' he asked contritely. 'You were standing by the wall and I went up to you and I said, "Could I have the honour?" And when we were coming home we walked down lovers' lane, where they had all the seats and the statues.'

'And you made a clown of yourself,' she said unforgivingly.

'Yes, didn't I just?' remembering how he had climbed the statue in the moonlight to show off. From the top of it he could see the Clyde, the ships and the cranes.

'And remember the flicks?' he said. 'We used tae get in wi jam jars. And do you mind the man who used to come down the passage at the interval spraying us with disinfectant?'

The interior of the cinema came back to him in a warm flood: the children in the front rows keeping up a continual barrage of noise, the ushers hushing them, the smoke, the warmth, the pies slapping against faces, the carved cherubs in the flaking roof blowing their trumpets.

'You'd like that, wouldn't you?' she said. 'Remember it was me who drove you to the top.'

'Whit dae ye mean?' – like a bull wounded in the arena.

'You were lazy, that was what was wrong with you. You'd go out ferreting when you were here. You liked being with the boys.

'Nothing wrong with that. What's wrong wi that?'

'What do you want? That they should all wave flags? That all the dirty boys and girls should line the street with banners five miles high? They don't give a damn about you, you know that. They're all dead and rotting and we should be back in Africa where we belong.'

He heard the voices round him. It was New Year's Eve

and they were all dancing in a restaurant which had a fountain
in the middle, and in the basin hundreds of pennies.

'Knees up, Mother Brown,' Jamieson was shouting to
Hannah.

'You used to dance, too,' he said, 'on New Year's Night.'

'I saw old Manson dying in that room,' he said, pointing
at a window. The floor and the ceiling and the walls seemed to
have drops of perspiration and Manson had a brown flannel
cloth wrapped round his neck. He couldn't breathe. And he
heard the mice scuttering behind the walls.

She turned on him. 'What are you bringing that up for?
Why don't you forget it? Do you enjoy thinking about these
things?'

'Shut up,' he shouted, 'you didn't even have proper table
manners when I met you.'

She stalked out to the car and he stayed where he was. To
hell with her. She couldn't drive anyway.

He just wondered if anyone they had known still remained.
He climbed the stair quietly till he came to the door of their
old flat. No gaslight there now. On the door was written the
name 'Rafferty', and as he leaned down against the letter-box
he heard the blast of a radio playing a pop song.

He went down again quietly.

He thought of their own two rooms there once, the living-
room with the table, the huge Victorian wardrobe (which
was too big for the bedroom) and the huge Victorian dresser.

As he looked out of the close he saw that his car was
surrounded by a pack of children, his wife, sheltered behind
glass, staring ahead of her, an empress surrounded by prairie
dogs.

He rushed out. 'Hey,' he said, 'don't scratch my car.'

'Whit is it?' a hard voice shouted from above.

He looked up. 'Nothing,' he said, 'I was just telling them
not to scratch my car.'

'Why have you goat it there onyway?'

The woman was thin and stringy and wore a cheap bracelet round her throat. A bit like Mrs Jamieson but less self-effacing.

'I was just paying a visit,' he said. 'I used to live here.'

'They're no daeing onything to your caur,' said the voice which was like a saw that would cut through steel for ever.

'It's an expensive car,' he said, watching his wife who was sitting in it like a graven image, lips firmly pressed together.

Another window opened. 'Hey, you there! I'm on night shift. Let's get a bit of sleep. Right?'

A pair of hairy hands slammed the window down again.

Two tall youngsters chewing gum approached.

'Hey, mister, whit are you on about?' They stared at him, legs crossed, delicate narrow toes.

'Nice bus,' said the one with the long curving moustache.

'Nice bus, eh Charley?'

They moved forward in concert, a ballet.

'Look,' he began, 'I was just visiting.' Then he stopped. Should he tell them that he was a rich man who had made good? It might not be advisable. One of them absently kicked one of the front tyres and then suddenly said to his wife, 'Peek a boo'. She showed no sign that she had seen him. They reminded him of some Africans he had seen, insolent young toughs, town-bred.

'All right, boys,' he said in an ingratiating voice. 'We're going anyway. We've seen all we want.'

'Did you hear that, Micky? He's seen all he wants to see. Would you say that was an insult?' Micky gazed benevolently at him through a lot of hair.

'Depends. What have you seen, daddy?'

'I used to live here,' he said jovially. 'In the old days. The best years of my life.' The words rang hollow between them.

'Hear that?' said Micky. 'Hear him. He's left us. Daddy's left us.'

He came up close and said quietly,

Get out of here, daddy, before we cut you up, and take

your camera and your bus with you. And your bag too. Right?'

The one with the curving moustache spat and said quietly 'Tourist.'

He got into the car beside his still unsmiling wife who was still staring straight ahead of her. The car gathered speed and made its way down the main street. In the mirror he could see the brown tenement diminishing. The thin stringy woman was still at the window looking out, screaming at the children.

The shops along both sides of the street were all changed. There used to be a road down to the river and the lavatories but he couldn't see anything there now. Later on he passed a new yellow petrol-station, behind a miniature park with a blue bench on it.

'Mind we used to take the bus out past here?' he said, looking towards the woods on their right, where all the secret shades were, and the squirrels leaped.

The sky was darkening and the light seemed concentrated ahead of them in steely rays.

Suddenly he said,

'I wish to God we were home.'

She smiled for the first time. But he was still thinking of the scarred tenement and of what he should have said to these youths. Punks. He should have said, 'This is my home too. More than yours. You're just passing through.'

Punks with Edwardian moustaches. By God, if they were in Africa they would be sorted out. A word in the ear of the Chief Inspector over a cigar and that would be it. By God, they knew how to deal with punks where he came from.

He thought of razor-suited Jamieson setting out on a Friday night in his lone battle with the Catholics. Where was he now? Used to be a boiler-man or something. By God, he would have sorted them out. And his wife used to clean the cinema steps on those big draughty winter days.

'So you admit you were wrong,' said his wife.

He drove on, accelerating past a smaller car and blaring his horn savagely. There was no space in this bloody country. Everybody crowded together like rats.

'Here, look at that,' he said, 'that didn't use to be there.' It was a big building, probably a hospital.

'Remember we used to come down here on the bus,' he said. 'That didn't use to be there.'

He drove into the small town and got out of the car to stretch. The yellow lights rayed the road and the cafés had red globes above them. He could hardly recognize the place.

'We'd better find a hotel,' he said.

His wife's face brightened.

They stopped at the Admiral and were back home when the boy in the blue uniform with the yellow edgings took their rich brown leather cases. People could be seen drinking in the bar which faced directly on to the street. They were standing about with globes of whisky in their hands. He recognized who they were. They had red faces and red necks, and they stood there decisively as if they belonged there. Their wives wore cool gowns and looked haggard and dissipated.

His own wife put her hand in his as they got out of the car. Now she was smiling and trailing her fur coat. She walked with a certain exaggerated delicacy. It looked as if it might be a good evening after all. He could tell the boys about his sentimental journey, it would make a good talking point, they would get some laughs from it. No, on second thoughts perhaps not. He'd say something about Scotland anyway, and not forget to make sure that they got to know how well he had done.

The two of them walked in. 'Waiter,' he said loudly, 'two whiskies with ice.' Some of them looked at him, then turned away again. That waiter should have his hair cut. After a few whiskies they would gravitate into the neighbourhood of the others, those men who ran Scotland, the backbone of the nation. People like himself. By God, less than him. He had had the guts to travel.

Outside it was quite dark. Difficult to get used to this climate. His wife was smiling as if she expected someone to photograph her.

Now she was home. In a place much like Africa, the bar of a first class hotel.

He took out a cigar to show who he was, and began to cut it. In the lights pouring out from the hotel he could see his car bulging like a black wave.

He placed his hand over his wife's and said,

'Well, dear, it's been a tiring day.'

With a piercing stab of pain he recalled Africa, the drinkers on the veranda, the sky large and open and protective, the place where one knew where one was, among Europeans like oneself.

To have found one's true home was important after all. He sniffed his whisky, swirling it around in the goblet, golden and clear and thin and burningly pure.

TALKING POINTS

1. In the opening paragraphs the author contrasts the opulence of the couple with the meanness of the surroundings. Pick out details that bring out the contrast; but also add a note on the similarities traced between the surroundings and the appearance of the couple.
2. The flashback to the story of the factor comes as the first big personal climax. What does this memory tell us about the character and attitude of the man?
3. The confrontation with the youngsters introduces a note of menace into the story. In what sense can this part be regarded as the climax; and what commentary does it make about society today?
4. The arrival of the couple at the hotel at the end of the story is presented as a return home. Consider the use of the word 'home' here, in the title, and in the structure of the story generally.
5. 'Man is romantic, woman a realist.' Comment on this in the light of the story.
6. Comment on the irony in the contrast between the man's picture of himself and the picture he actually presents to the reader.
7. What commentary does the story make about human life?

Ian Hamilton Finlay (b. 1925)

THE MONEY

At one period in my life, as a result of the poverty I was suffering, it became impossible for me to tell a lie. Consequently, I became the recipient of National Assistance money. But it all began when I applied for Unemployment Benefit money at the little Labour Exchange in the nearest town.

As I entered the building, the typist turned to the clerk and I heard her whisper, 'The artist is here again.' No, she gave me a capital – 'Artist.' The clerk rose, and, making no attempt to attend to me, crossed to the door marked 'Welfare Officer' and gave it a knock.

The clerk was seated. Presently the Welfare Officer appeared. He is, or I should say, was then, a rather stout, unhappy looking person in his early forties. This afternoon, as if he had known I was coming to see him, he wore a fashionable sports jacket and a large, arty and gaudy tie. My heart went out to him as he advanced towards the counter saying: 'I've told you before. We have no jobs for you. You are simply wasting our time.'

Somehow, I had got myself into a ridiculous *lolling* position, with my elbows on the counter and my hand supporting my chin. I gazed up at the Welfare Officer and replied timidly, 'I haven't come about a job. I have *been* in a job. Now I have come to ask you for Unemployment Benefit money.'

As I spoke, I could not help glancing at the large, locked safe that stood in the far corner of the room. Out of it, distinctly, a curious silence trickled, rather as smoke trickles out of the stove in my cottage. I had no doubt it was the silence of The Money I had just referred to.

'What!' exclaimed the Welfare Officer, raising his black, bushy eyebrows. 'You have been in a job!'

I nodded. 'I was editing a magazine.'

'And may I ask what salary you received?' he said, his tone disguising the question as an official one.

'One pound, three and sixpence,' I answered, for, as I explained, I could not tell a lie.

'Per month?' he suggested.

'Per week,' I replied with dignity. 'And it was only a part-time job.'

'Hum! In that case, assuming that you have been in part-time employment and did not leave it of your own accord you will be entitled to claim part-time Unemployment Benefit money from this Labour Exchange,' he informed me, all in one breath.

'What? But that isn't fair!' I retorted. My cheeks crimsoned; I took my elbows off the counter and waved my hands. 'That isn't just! I paid *full-time* National Insurance money. So I should draw *full-time* Unemployment Benefit money from this Labour Exchange!'

My impassioned outburst brought a nervous titter from the typist and an astonished rustle from the young clerk. The Welfare Officer, however, only glanced at me for an instant, turned his back on me, strode into his office and shut the door.

I waited a few moments. Then, 'Do you think I have offended him?' I asked the clerk. 'Am I supposed to go away now? Do you know?'

But, before I had received an answer to my unhappy question, the Welfare Officer appeared once more, bearing two large volumes – no, *tomes*, in his arms. CRASH! He dropped the tomes on the counter, right under my nose.

Then he opened one of the tomes; and slowly, silently, with brows sternly knitted, he began to thumb his way through the

thick and closely printed sheets. Page 100 . . . Page 250. . . .
And he still had the second of the tomes in reserve.

I moistened my lips, and said weakly, 'Very well, I give in.
I am only entitled to draw part-time Unemployment money
from this Labour Exchange.'

'That is correct,' observed the Welfare Officer. Closing the
tome, and flexing his muscles, he bent to push it aside. Then he
took a step or two towards the safe. That, at least, was my
impression. Looking back on the incident, I see that he was
really going to the cupboard to fetch forms.

But the sight of his too-broad figure retreating to fetch me
The Money touched my heart. True, he had won a hollow
victory, but I did not mind, and I wanted him to know I did
not mind.

'Thank you,' I said, in low, sincere tones.

The Welfare Officer stopped at once. He turned to face
me again. 'Thank you? Why are you saying thank you? You
haven't got the money yet, you know,' he warned me.

'I know that,' I said, and I apologized to him. He appeared
to accept my apology, and, turning, took another step or two
towards the cupboard – or, as *I* thought, the safe.

Again I was touched. It was the combination of my poverty,
his pathetic appearance in his rich clothes, and the thought of
The Money he was about to give me. It was as if he was
generously giving it to me out of his own pocket, I felt.

'But honestly,' I sighed, 'I'm awfully grateful to you. You
see, if you give me The Money, I'll be able to work . . . I'll be
free to work – at last!'

'Work? What work?' exclaimed the Welfare Officer. He
halted, flew into a rage, and once more turned to face me. 'If
you are going to be working you cannot claim Unemployment Benefit money! Don't you understand that!' he shouted.

At this moment, the typist intervened, saying, 'He doesn't
mean work. What he means is, taking pictures. Like that one
– I forget his name – who cut off his ear.'

I, too, flew into a rage, and not only at this mention of *ears*.

'*Taking* pictures? TAKING pictures? PAINTING pictures if you don't mind!' I fixed the typist with my eye, and as a sort of reflex action, she bent forward and typed several letters on her machine. Then, looking at the Welfare Officer, I asked: 'Just tell me, yes, do tell me, how is a person to work when they are in a job? I can only work when I am NOT in a job! When I am in a job I CANNOT work, do you understand?'

'Are you working or are you not working?' shouted the exasperated Welfare Officer at the very top of his voice. 'Think it over will you, and let me know!'

So I thought it over, and that very night, by the light of my oil lamp, I wrote a polite letter to the authorities in the Labour Exchange. In effect, what I said was: 'I resign.' And the following morning, I handed the letter to the postman when he delivered the bills at my mountain-cottage.

But in the afternoon, when I was painting in my kitchen, I happened to look through the window, and I saw a neat little man. Clothed in a pin-striped office-suit and clasping a brief-case, he was clinging rather breathlessly to the fence. Several sheep had ceased to crop the hillside and were gazing at him with evident surprise.

As he did not look like a shepherd, I at once concluded that he must be – could only be – an art-dealer. Overjoyed, I thrust my hairless brushes back in their jam-pot, threw the door open, and ran out into the warm summer sunshine to make him welcome.

My collie dog, swinging the shaggy pendulum of his tail, and barking furiously, preceded me. 'Don't be afraid!' I shouted to the art-dealer. However, he had already scrambled back over the fence, and was standing, at bay, in the shade of the wood.

Calling the dog off, I opened the gate, and, smiling,

advanced to meet him with outstretched hand. 'Good afternoon. I'm very glad to see you,' I said. The art-dealer took my hand, shook it warmly, and replied, 'I am from the National Assistance Board. Good afternoon.'

It was then I noticed he had been holding *forms*. The collie still bounded about us, leaping up on the stranger so as to sniff his interesting office-y smells. 'Fin McCuil,' I ordered, 'you mustn't touch *those*. Bad. Go away, now. Chew your bone instead!'

Then I turned to the National Assistance man, and I explained to him, with many apologies, that I had resigned.

He listened sympathetically, but when I had finished speaking, he came a step nearer to me, placed his arm around my shoulder, and said softly, 'Son, there is no need to feel like that, you are perfectly entitled to take this money.'

He tapped his brief-case. He meant, of course, the National Assistance money.

'But I don't feel *like that*,' I assured him. 'Believe me, I feel grateful . . . I mean, ungrateful . . . bringing you all this way . . . But I have resigned . . . I don't think I fit in very well, you see . . .'

'Son,' said the National Assistance man, speaking as no art-dealer ever did, 'I understand your position. No, don't look surprised. I do understand it. For you see, my own brother is a violinist —' And breaking off for a moment, he gazed thoughtfully down the steep and rickety old path up to my house. Here was a green, ferny landing; there a hole in the banisters of bracken where a sheep had crashed through. 'He lives in a garret,' he continued. 'He is in the same . . . er . . . position . . . you see, as you are. He sits up there all day playing his violin.'

So there had been a mistake. It was just as I thought, and almost as bad as if I had told a lie. 'But I don't play the violin,' I pointed out. 'I don't play anything. You see, there's been a mistake.'

'No, no, I understand. You don't play the violin. You paint pictures,' said the National Assistance man soothingly. 'By the way,' he added, 'what do you do with them?'

'Do with them?' I repeated, at a loss. 'Ah, do with them: I see. Well, the big ones I put upstairs, in the attic. The little ones I put downstairs, in the cupboard.'

'You don't ever think of selling them?' he asked gently.

'Selling them! HA, HA! No, I don't,' I said, delighted by the fantasy of the question.

There was a pause. Suddenly he looked me straight in the eye, and he asked me, point-blank, 'Son, do you want this money?'

I could not tell a lie. 'I do,' I said.

So he thrust his hand into his brief-case. He offered me The Money, and, without looking at It, I put It in my pocket as fast as I could. Money is a great embarrassment when you are poor.

'Just fill those in,' he explained.

So, I thought to myself, they are not pound notes; they are postal-orders. But when we had shaken hands and said good-bye to each other, I found they were no postal-orders, either; they were forms . . .

And I filled them in. And thereafter, till my truthfulness got me into fresh trouble (for, of course, I had been brought up to look on charity as trouble) they sent me a regular weekly cheque. For my part, I was requested to fill in a form stating what Employment I had undertaken during the week and how much money I had earned by it. As painting was not Employment, though it was Work, I very carefully wrote the words 'None' and 'Nil' in the appropriate columns. After five or six weeks they gave me a seven-shilling rise.

Then I sold a picture. And I was inspected at the same time by an unfamiliar National Assistance man.

It was a breezy, blue and golden day in early autumn when he arrived at the door of my cottage. No sooner had I answered his knock than he cheerfully apologized. 'Sorry, old chap. Can't wait long today. Two ladies down in the car . . .'

'I expect you are going out for a picnic,' I observed, wondering if I ought or ought not to return his wink.

'Ha, ha, old boy, you are quite right there!' he answered.

'Well, do come in for just a moment,' I said. 'I shan't keep you, I promise.'

Lifting my easel out of the way, and hastily removing my wet palette from a chair, I invited him into my kitchen, and he sat down. On my palette, as it happened. He had sat on the chair on to which I had removed it; I at once ran for the turpentine and the cloth.

When we had cleaned him up, I put in tentatively: 'There is something I wanted to ask you. It's . . . er . . . it's about those . . . er . . . forms . . .'

'Forms?' His bright face clouded over. I was spoiling his picnic with my Prussian blue paint and my silly questions.

'Those . . . er . . . weekly forms that you send me . . .'

'Oh, those. You mean that you complete those, do you?' He seemed astonished that I did.

But I could not tell a lie. 'I'm afraid I do,' I confessed. 'Do you think it matters very much?'

'Ah, well, no harm done, I suppose.'

'Then there is a difficulty,' I announced. And quickly, so as not to keep the ladies waiting, I mentioned the awful problem I was now faced with. Painting, I explained, was not Employment, though it was *Work*. And even if I stretched a point and called it Employment, still it was not employment undertaken *this week*. The picture I had sold had been painted a whole year ago . . . How was I to inform them of the money I had received for it?

'I want to be quite truthful, you see,' I added. 'The form applies only to the present week . . . So, you see, it is difficult to be truthful.'

'If you want my advice, old boy, *be* truthful,' he answered.

'Yes, be truthful, that is always best. Or nearly always best, eh? HA, HA! Ah, hmm . . .' He rose, and moved to the door. 'I say,' he whispered to me, 'do I smell of turpentine?'

I sniffed at him, and assured him that he did not. 'The very best of luck then, old chap.' We shook hands. Halting to wave to me at frequent intervals, he hurried down the path, and I returned to the house.

There and then, determined to be truthful at all costs, I set about filling in my weekly form. 'Employment Undertaken – None.' And under 'Money Earned.' I carefully wrote – '£5. 5. 0.' It had, I reflected, that slight suggestion of paradox one expects with the truth.

I posted the form, and, by return of post, I was sternly summoned to the central office of the National Assistance Board.

When I entered the building, and gave my name at the desk, I was at once led, like a very special sort of person, down several long passages and into a room. There, I was awaited. Several men, all of whom, it was plain, were awaiting me, were seated rather grimly around a table. On the table lay my form. Strange to say, it looked completely different there; *absurd*.

On my arriving in the room, one of the men – their spokesman or perhaps the head one – pointed to my form, and said, 'What is *that*?'

'That? Why, it's my weekly form,' I replied.

'Can you explain it to us?' another asked me.

'Yes, easily,' I answered. And I proceeded to explain it to them. Time. Money. Work. Truth. When I had completed my explanation, one of them got up from his chair and fetched a tome. It was a signal, for, at this, they all left their chairs and fetched back tomes. They threw them open on the table.

I grew nervous. After a while, I looked at the one who had first addressed me, and, pointing to his tome, I said, 'You are wasting your time. *I am not in it.*' He looked at me, but he did not smile or reply.

'Gentlemen —,' I began, interrupting them. 'Gentlemen, I think it would be best if I gave up The Money. I don't quite fit in, I quite see that. I sympathize with you. So I resign.'

At this, there was a sudden and very noticeable change in the atmosphere. They were obviously relieved at my decision. They smiled at me. But one of them said: 'There is no need to be hasty.' And another added: 'We wish you well.'

'Then I am to go on taking The Money, am I?' I asked.

But once more there was a change in the atmosphere. The men became grim again, and put on frowns.

'I see,' I said. 'Then I have no alternative but to resign.'

Smiles. Relief. Opening of silver cigarette-cases. 'There is no need to be hasty.' 'We wish you well.'

'I believe you,' I assured them. 'Will you send on the forms or shall I just fill them in now?'

'Now!' said the men, speaking all at once.

So I completed the forms of resignation, and I left the building a free man.

TALKING POINTS

1. The first episode takes place in the Labour Exchange and centres on two arguments between the artist and the official. Outline these, and say what light they shed on the narrator's character.
2. The second episode takes place in the artist's home in a more relaxed atmosphere. Discuss the humorous touches that help to develop further the impression of the narrator as an odd person.
3. The third episode, involving the visit of an unfamiliar National Assistance man to the artist's home, develops the comedy and the dilemma still further. Illustrate the comedy in this scene; and explain and comment on the 'awful problem' the narrator was faced with.
4. The story reaches its climax and resolution in the final scene in the office of the National Assistance Board. Consider how the author achieves his effects of comic drama, tension and relaxation here; and discuss the implication behind the last words – 'I left the building a free man'.
5. The rational individualist against the logical bureaucratic system – what laughter arises from this clash and what commentary is thereby made on the nature of man in society?

Robin Jenkins (b. 1912)

FLOWERS

At the door of the little school Miss Laing frowned at her seven scholars off to gather flowers.

'Can I trust you?' she asked.

'Yes, miss,' they chorused, except one.

Miss Laing pointed a chubby stern finger at the red-eyed dissenter.

'Now, Margaret, I want no more nonsense from you.' She gazed with professional intentness at the small sulky girl with the red ribbon in her hair. 'Do you understand?'

Huffishly, Margaret nodded.

'That's a good girl. Now off with you. Come back at once when I ring the bell.'

As the teacher stood at the door in the heat and brilliance of the sun, watching the children scamper to the gate, a great roar was heard growing louder and louder until in front, low over the sea loch, with the pilots clearly visible, three fighter aeroplanes in camouflage paint flashed into view, flying with exhilarating swiftness and power.

Miss Laing was exhilarated. She waved her hand wildly.

'There they are, children,' she cried. 'There are the true flowers of our country, the most precious, the most beautiful. Wave to them.'

The children were startled and even a little alarmed by her excessive white-haired enthusiasm. Aeroplanes were now commonplace on the loch. Canna Rock was used for bombing practice. That was why almost every day they had all to promise solemnly, with their hands on their Bibles, never to go down to the shore.

Then the aeroplanes were gone again and their roar faded until a bee buzzing by was louder.

'Remember,' cried Miss Laing. 'Be very careful.'

Margaret halted in the shade of a tall pine and watched the others hurrying towards the fields at Laggan under the larch wood, away from the sea. She sneered as she saw how Roderick McKenzie's long thin lassie-like legs twinkled under his torn kilt; he had his little sister Morag by the hand. They all gabbled to one another in Gaelic, mysterious and hateful to her Lowland ears.

Tears came into her eyes. She looked about her and saw, with aversion, the bell heather streaming like fire along the top of the dyke, the red branches and velvety foliage of the pine overhead, and the tiny school with its queer high roof. She wished to see the shops, houses, tramcars of home. She wished this summer afternoon to be playing in Mathieson Street with her friends Belzie Carruthers and Janet Morrison. She didn't want to be here in the Highlands staying with Aunt Sheena. She didn't want to be safe from bombs.

It was silly anyhow picking wild flowers in the hot sunshine. Miss Laing would just show off by telling their names, and then she'd either throw them out or else put them into a vase where in a day they'd wither.

Suddenly she jumped up over the dyke and ran across the heather. She didn't crouch nor try to hide. She didn't care if Miss Laing was spying on her. She didn't care either that she was breaking a sacred promise.

The sea was in sight with gold and silver spangles swimming in it like wonderful swans when she abruptly stopped, drawing in her breath in astonishment and awe. On a rock lay neatly coiled a small adder, green with gold and black zig-zag markings; its little head, eyes shut, formed the apex of the coil. It lay sunning itself, camouflaged against the background of greeny-grey lichened stone and gently waving fronds of bracken.

She didn't know what to do. Adders, Miss Laing had warned them, were dangerous and must always be avoided. There was plenty of room for her to creep safely past. But she hesitated, and the snake awoke, conscious of her presence. It raised its head high, glancing quickly round. She saw its tiny eyes and its black tongue spitting in and out.

Suddenly it seemed to represent not only that detestable alien country but her own wickedness in disobeying. Furiously she lifted a stone and threw it. The snake hissed and slithered away. She snatched up a stick of hazel and stepped in pursuit, striking again and again though she felt sick with fear and hatred. A lucky blow crushed its head against a stone and blood trickled from its mouth; but it still hissed and slithered on, escaping into the bracken. She stood gazing at the speck of blood and scraped it with her stick. She was amazed because she hadn't thought a snake would have red blood in it.

She became aware of a yellow flower at her feet. Like the serpent it seemed hateful for some reason she could not understand, and she was about to trample on it when, un-accountably, its beauty, harmlessness, and its loneliness there amidst the tall brackens, moved her instead to stoop, tenderly pluck it, and hold it against her cheek.

Such obscure intensity of feeling was a new experience for her, and she stood gazing in fascination and guilt along the seaweeded rock and white sand. A black and white bird with long red legs and beak rose up with shrill cries. She watched it in fear. Then she looked again at a sandy corner among the rocks. Perhaps she might be able to paddle there. Would there be any unexploded bombs or ferocious crabs or stinging jellyfish?

She came down the bank cautiously and, flower in hand, walked slowly across the beach. The cool salty breeze was pleasant on her face and legs. More birds rose and screamed. She waited till they were gone.

When she crept round the boulder that shut off the sandy nook she stopped, surprised and embarrassed. It had never occurred to her there might be someone there.

Two men were lying stretched out on the sand in the shallow glittering water.

It was a strange place to lie, especially as they seemed to have their clothes on. She watched them moving gently with the waves' push. The water surely must be very warm. Certainly the sun struck it with a great blaze, forcing her to shade her eyes with her hand.

Smiling shyly, uncertain of her welcome, she started to walk over to them.

She paused again suddenly when she was close enough to see they wore airmen's clothing: they had the huge fur-lined boots, though one of them seemed to have only one boot on. They gave no sign at all that they knew she was there. Further along the beach the red-beaked birds screamed again. She walked a step or two nearer, then rigidly halted. Her scalp tingled and her whole body seemed frozen in the cold bright sea. In her hand the yellow flower was crushed into a green and black mess.

One of the airmen, with fair hair, had no face at all: while the other's face was half gone, and what remained was unrecognizable as human. The one with the single boot had only one leg; the fingers of his right hand, flung out in the shallow water, were gleaming bones. A sweet nasty smell mingled with the tang of the sea.

Screaming she turned and raced back. Frenzied eagerness to shock Miss Laing with the news of her discovery drove her on as much as the horror itself. But as she made to clamber up the bank she became aware of the crushed flower in her hand. Weeping and yelling, she rubbed it madly on the grass.

TALKING POINTS

1. In the first sequence of this story, the narrative gradually focuses on the figure of Margaret and at the same time sketches in the setting. How does the author use the setting to sharpen the impressions of the girl's reactions and rebellious mood?

2. What exactly happens in the final sequence? How does the author build up to and present the terrible moment of recognition? (A consideration of film technique may help here.)

3. What, separately, do the adder, the flower and the airmen contribute to the human experience?

4. Consider Jenkins's method of leading in to his story (his introduction) and his method of phasing out (his conclusion).

5. What clue does the title 'Flowers' give us as to the tone or attitude of the author? What is its full significance in human terms?

Margaret Hamilton (1915-1972)

JENNY STAIRY'S HAT

Neighbours had often seen the bowler hat as they stood at the door, waiting for Jenny to bring a morsel of sugar or marge, to be paid back out of next week's rations. Jenny kept herself to herself, and never would ask you in, though her house must be tidy enough, old maid that she was, with never a man or bairn coming in to mess things.

'I see you've your young man in, Jenny,' they said, winking at the hat hanging up in the lobby.

On the way downstairs they would laugh at the idea of Jenny Stairy with a man – her in that old coat that fitted where it touched her because she had got it second-hand from a customer. Somebody had once said the coat came out of the Ark and Jenny came with it – as the female ostrich.

There was no doubt in anyone's mind that the hat had belonged to one of Jenny's brothers and she kept it to scare off burglars.

But Jenny, owning nothing of value, was not afraid of thieves, and the hat, ancient and curly-brimmed, would have deceived no one.

The hat belonged to a time when Jenny was not a stairy, but young Jenny McFadyen, selling pipeclay and pails to other people from behind the ironmonger's counter. It was not a shop where lads had much reason to come in for chaff, but somehow they found their way there.

'I'll cairry up ma mither's paraffin, Jenny.'

'Whaur's your bottle?'

'Ach, I'll hae to come back wi' it the morn.'

Then, her slenderness had not turned to gauntness, and her hair, now so thin and scraped, was a soft light crown above her face. It was a peaked, inscrutable face, with brown eyes which made men try to follow her at night if they caught a glimpse of her in the gaslight of the street. And, with it all, she was a douce-looking creature whom you could take home to your mother and be sure of a welcome for her as your intended.

But none of the young men who came about the shop was ever allowed to take Jenny home, or even walk out with her. They were too much like her own brothers – and besides there was Peter Abercromby.

Peter worked in a lawyer's office. He had spoken to Jenny at the corner one night, asked her the way to somewhere in such a refined voice that she answered. While he was seeing her home, she discovered that he lived with his mother only a few blocks away.

Every Saturday night after that he was waiting for her when the shop closed. Minnie Walker from the draper's next door used to tease half-jealously if Jenny and she came out together.

'My, some folks is fair gettin' up in the world – I'll need to tell the chaps they've nae chance wi' their bunnets an' dungarees!' she would cry a shade too loudly, so that Jenny, going forward to take Peter's arm in his navy-blue suit, would be certain he had heard.

But he never gave any sign. Precisely he raised his bowler hat and said, 'Good evening, Jenny. What's your news?'

There was never any. At least, she couldn't tell him what old McNair the ironmonger had said yesterday to the woman who was buying a chamber-pot, or how the other night, washing the window, she had been so afraid that . . .

So she always said, 'Oh, nothing much, Peter. What's *your* news?'

He would set off primly on an account of how something

had gone missing in the office, and he, Peter, had miraculously been able to find it.

Then the inevitable: 'My mother's been not so well.'

Jenny had never seen his mother, but she came to know her as a woman always at death's door, but never quite being pulled through. Peter was her only child, and Jenny sometimes wondered how she would get on, looking after his mother, when, if. . . . Or would theirs be one of those courtships which went on for years, waiting for the man's mother to die?

Because of his bowler hat and navy suit, Jenny could never be sure of anything. Walking with him through the streets, she would feel sick with waiting for the moment when he judged it dark enough to put his arm round her.

Sometimes she edged him towards a doorway, but he steered firmly away, talking all the time.

'I was reading in the papers. About this Irish home rule . . .'

When he talked of what he read in the papers, his mouth became a peashooter, sending out the words in self-righteous little bursts. It was a firm mouth that could kiss rather well, except that he took it away too soon.

In winter Jenny took him home for his supper. The McFadyens lived on the top flat, in a room and kitchen – Tom and Jim and Jenny and their father and mother. With them all in the kitchen it was a crush for supper, because Tom and Jim were big loud men, and Peter used to turn pale and a little shrewish, sitting with his tea in his hand.

Once they almost came to blows over Irish home rule, because Jim and Tom had Irish mates in the shipyard where they worked and they wouldn't believe what Peter had read in the papers.

'A lot of ignoramuses!' Peter was saying, with angry foam on his lips.

'What did you say, mister?' Jim got to his feet, putting down his cup.

From the other side Tom lumbered over, and Peter, smallish at the best of times, looked like a midge between two bulls.

'Peter – your tea's out!' Jenny plunged in at the more dangerous side, which was Jim's, and by questions about milk and sugar, to which she knew the answers, created a diversion long enough to save the peace.

She got her mother to 'speak to' Tom and Jim, and they began to go out on Saturday nights. Jim had a girl called Isa Bain, and Tom could always find pals at a street corner.

'Is Lord Muck awa'?' they would ask, coming in on pretended tip-toe. 'Can a chap get into his ain hoose?'

With Jim and Tom out, Peter talked away happily. Jenny, gripped by a merciless longing for the few minutes when she would have Peter to herself, saying good night on the stair, had less than usual to say. Her mother ignored Peter, as she did everyone, because she was too tired to notice. But her father would listen, smiling now and then with a strange sweetness behind his moustache. His smile was a sign of weakness, but you loved him for it – or Jenny did.

'Ach Faither, you're hopeless!' was the worst you could ever say to him, and sometimes only the fact that he was there made life in the cramped flat seem worth while.

'We'll need to get you out of all this,' Peter murmured one night on the stairhead.

'Him and his *all this*!' thought Jenny, too indignant to feel exalted by this near proposal.

Then he kissed her and she forgot everything except the hope that he would kiss her again. But he never did, and tonight as usual he withdrew his arm and pattered down the long stairs. She listened to hear the last of his rubber soles on the two front steps of the close.

Jenny did most of the housework because her mother was often in bed. She did not suffer from 'nerves' as Peter's mother did. Her body had been distorted at the birth of Jim, her second child; she had gone on to have a third and fourth, who died, and a fifth, Jenny, who miraculously lived.

Jenny minded none of the work except the windows. Sometimes, if Jim were out, she could get Tom to wash them. But, if both brothers were in, they would sit, one on each side of the fire, with their feet on the hob, and Jenny would grit her teeth as she sat or stood on the window-sills, not daring to look down, yet doing it in case she would forget how high she was.

She enjoyed washing down the stairs, moving down the long flight on her knees, with her pail and clayey water. When she was almost finished she liked to look up and see the top steps already dry and clean, except for the footmark which was certain to have been left by a Docherty child, slithering up to the house next door.

Sometimes her father would come up, unsteady because he had been drinking. Jenny, hearing his first dragging steps in the close, would leave her pail and go running to help him.

'You're a good lass, Jenny,' he always insisted all the way up.

Neighbours, though they heard, thought little about it, for old McFadyen was a painter – a trade that gave you a thirst if anything did. But they wondered what his daughter felt about it, her that was supposed to be making such a good match for herself.

Jenny was used to it as part of her father, the weakness that made her love him. Cleaning the stair lavatory after he had been sick, she would grow angry and resolve to give him a tongueing, but when she came in and saw the bowed man, looking so miserable, with the thin streaks of hair across his head, it would all boil down to 'Ach, Faither, you're hopeless!'

Peter Abercromby was a teetotaller and Jenny respected him for it. But she sometimes wondered whether a dram wouldn't make him more – well . . .

Peter's mother died at last. Jenny saw the notice in the paper and knew that this, more than any kissing on the stair, would bring matters to a head.

He did not come to meet her that Saturday. It was not to be wondered at, since it was the day after the funeral. All through the following week, by an effort of will, she kept herself away from his house. It was not her 'place' to go unless he asked her, but she had sent a letter of sympathy with an offer to 'perform any service whatsoever within my power to assist you in bearing this grievous burden of sorrow which has descended upon you (and yours)' – copying it word for word from a book in case she would make mistakes.

On Friday night he came to see her. She was dusting in the room and it was Jim who went to the door.

'Here's Lord Muck!' he called loudly, but Jenny, her fingers plucking feverishly at her apron strings as she rushed to bring Peter in, was not at all bothered.

They sat on the sofa, inches apart. Peter was nervous and played with his hat, suspended awkwardly between his navy-blue knees. She ought to have taken it from him, she . . .

'Thank you for your letter, Jenny.'

'Your mother, did she . . . ?'

He told her about it. The sudden pain, the doctor, the ambulance. The operation but it was too late. Appendicitis. To think it should have carried her off after the years of suffering she had had with other things.

There seemed to be nothing more to say. Of course he would not have had time to read the papers since. . . . But he was beginning as usual:

'I was reading in the papers. About an Archduke who's been murdered. It may mean war for France. But it would be foolish for this country to . . .'

He went on in normal peashooter fashion. She could hear Jim's and Tom's voices raised angrily, then the slam of the kitchen door. The two of them slept in the parlour and they had an early rise in the morning. If only Peter would hurry.

She knew what he had come for. It was not very decent so soon after his mother's death, but what was a man to do with a two-room-and-kitchen house and no woman to clean and look after him?

At last he was saying: 'Jenny, we've ... ep ... been going steady ... ep ... for two years now. I was wondering ...'

Jenny waited. Surely tonight he would kiss her twice, surely now she would be free of the doubt that made her afraid to open her mouth in case an uncouth word would shatter everything between them.

'So, Jenny, I thought maybe ...'

Jim and Tom burst in without knocking.

'Coortin's feenished fur the nicht, mister!'

'Awa' hame to your bed an' we'll get to oors!'

Jim caught him under the oxters and Tom seized his feet.

His voice beat punily against their muscular strength. Jenny caught at his arm as it clutched the air.

'Jim an' Tom ... pit him doon ... are ye no' ashamed o' yoursel's ... pit him doon!'

Tom dropped his feet for an instant to open the outside door but Peter could not get his balance in time and he was lifted again and dumped on the mat outside.

'Oh, Peter, you'll need to mind they're rough craters – no' like you. They didny mean ony hairm ...'

Peter picked himself up, dusted his trousers and mopped his mouth for a high-pitched parting shot:

'You'll hear from my solicitors!'

Afterwards they found his hat on the parlour floor and they hung it in the lobby in case he would come back for it.

Jenny told Minnie Walker about it. She had to tell someone, for it got worse with bottling up. This was Monday, and Peter hadn't shown up on the Saturday and there had been a long dead Sunday between.

Minnie was sympathetic. She was a squat, dark girl, and,

although her mother owned the draper's shop where she worked, it didn't seem likely that she would ever get a husband.

'Thae men!' she said vehemently. 'Oh my God, Jenny, is it no' terrible whit they can dae to ye?'

Then the cut meant as comfort:

'Ach, ye're weel rid o' him if he doesny think enough o' ye to come back.'

That was what her mother said, it was what any decent girl ought to feel especially if she had plenty of boys eager to take Peter's place. But Jenny felt only part of it: he hadn't cared enough to come back.

The next Saturday, before shop closing time, she thought she saw him outside, pacing on the pavement as he always did. She hung back, afraid yet eager to go out. When at last she did, it was as if the blow had fallen all over again on a place already tender. The pavement was wet and empty. Even Minnie had closed her door early and was gone. Jenny walked home alone in the rain.

Things happened in the next few weeks. War began. Jim, having got Isa Bain into trouble, married her. Tom joined the H.L.I. and was sent to England.

Jenny lived through it, a little remote, none too hearty at Isa's wedding, but outwardly almost the same Jenny, steeling herself to wash the windows, and choking off the lads who came into the ironmonger's. Once she went for a walk with a boy in new khaki, but he was so shyly passionate and so like Tom that she ran away from him.

She took to washing the stairs on Saturday nights, and would pause, wringing her cloth, every time a rubber-soled foot fell on the close. Only when a downstairs door had banged or the inevitable Docherty child had slipped up past her, did she begin again, wiping in skilful semi-circles.

When she had finished each step, and before it was dry, she would take her pipeclay and at each side trace a row of loops, like a child's first attempt at writing. Mrs Docherty across the landing had no time for such fancywork, and every time Jenny's turn came round she had to trace her whirligigs afresh. But in the mornings she liked to see them gleaming, white against the grey stone, like a promise of something the day never brought.

Jim came up one night, alone, the stairs being too much for Isa with her time so near. He lifted Peter Abercromby's hat from its peg in the lobby and birled it into the kitchen.

'Ye needny be keepin' that ony mair.'

'How?'

'He can get yin oot o' stock. He's marryin' Minnie Walker next week.'

It must be true enough, because Isa's mother lived next door to the Walkers.

Jenny went to wash the stair. It was not her turn, but the stair was the only place where she could be alone.

Savagely she slapped her cloth back and forward. Minnie Walker with her 'You're well rid of him . . .' She remembered the night when she had seen Peter outside and Minnie had been away so early . . . probably chaffing him as she locked the door, talking of Jenny and saying, 'You're well rid of *her*,' till he believed it and went with Minnie.

Minnie need never be unsure of Peter, because of her mother's money.

Far below in the close, feet were stumbling up the first few steps. Neighbours heard, and knew it was Willie McFadyen again, with a drop over much. But they listened in vain for Jenny coming down to help him.

He crept up, making a long slow job of each step. He stopped behind Jenny, but her cloth moved ruthlessly on.

'*Fule!*' she muttered tensely, thinking of that dirty job, tonight of all nights.

But he shuffled on past the lavatory and into the house.

When she went up there was no sign of him in the kitchen. She emptied her pail and, after a gurgle of water in the sink waste came Jim's voice saying to his mother: 'It's no' oor war – Tom wasny needin' to fash himsel'.'

Then the banging on the door . . . somebody screaming . . . 'Mrs McFadyen . . . your man's fell ower the windy!'

He was lying at the edge of the pavement with the empty pail a few yards from him and water trickling down the gutter.

'It was the pail I seen first,' said Mrs McLean, one stair up. 'An' then the puir man cam' efter it . . .'

Other neighbours were muttering something about 'a dirty shame, letting a drunk man wash a windy.'

They put a cushion under his head, and Jenny's mother was weeping stormily. She had been tired and silent for so long that it was a wonder to discover she could weep.

Jenny's tears gushed suddenly as they lifted him and his arms fell helplessly. He had done this for her because she had been angry and he loved her.

'Aye, it was the pail I seen first,' Mrs McLean was beginning for more of the neighbours.

'Could he no' have minded,' thought Jenny, lashing against her sobs, '*I washed it masel' last nicht!*'

Jenny came home one day and found her mother selling Peter Abercromby's hat to a rag woman at the door. Angrily, Jenny hung it up and sent the woman away.

'We're takin' nothin' frae him, d'ye hear?'

Her mother shrugged. 'Whaur's the money to come frae?'

There was good money in munition work, but the hours were long when you had housework to do as well.

So one evening, after she had finished at the ironmonger's, Jenny made her way to a part of the town where there were clean red tenements, occupied mainly by professional and business men with their families. She chose a close at random and climbed the first stair. Her feet longed to run back down the stair and all the way home. But she went on and chapped at a stained glass door.

'Were you wantin' anybody to wash the stairs?'

The woman came out . . . a full-bosomed personage, chewing the last bite of her tea, so that you could not read the expression on her face. Jenny shrank, but held her head up.

'D'you mean it, my girl?'

'Y–yes.'

'Oh, thank *goodness*! I was beginning to think I'd have to wash them myself.'

It was easy. The whole stair dropped like a plum into her lap, at three pence per landing, twice a week. Soon she had the close on either side as well. Charwomen had gone to munitions, and she could have had more work if she had been able to do it.

At first she pretended that people passing would think she was washing her own stair. She always said 'Good evening,' and gentlemen especially were profuse in their apologies for marking her steps.

One evening a little boy came calling, 'Jenny Stairy, Jenny Stairy!'

She turned as if to ward off a blow. But he was a nice little boy, whose daddy was fighting in France, and he only wanted to know why the stair dried white after she had made it black with her wet cloth.

Soon afterwards Jenny gave up her work in the shop, and became a full-time stairy. Her mother had taken a shock which left her paralysed down one side, and Jenny could not be away from her for more than a few hours at a time.

Jenny Stairy became a familiar figure in her own street and in the district where she worked – a skinny creature with her hair pulled back, because she had no time for frizzing, and hands and feet made ungainly by the chilblains which were a result of washing stairs and closes in all weathers.

She had a routine rather than a life: getting up in the morning, attending to her mother, going to work, coming back to attend to her mother, going to work, coming back. Sometimes people wanted her to clean house for them, but she would not do it in case she would not please them or they would ask her to wash windows. She stuck to her routine, day in, day out, for years.

Once at New Year she put whirligigs on a close, but the lady asked her not to do it again, it made the place look so common. On Jenny's own stair the whorls still gleamed in the morning, like symbols of hope not dead.

There was a man called Ibbets, whom she saw every Tuesday and Friday. He was a foreman carpenter who had strayed into that quarter because of war wages and the scarcity of houses, and there had been quite a sensation at the time, because the 'tone' of the place was supposed to be lowered. But as tenants the Ibbets were peaceful enough, and it was not long before a neighbour was handing Jenny the pail and pipeclay for Mrs Ibbets, who was said to be 'not too well', with a significant tap of the forehead.

Because he lived so far from his work, John Ibbets was in for his dinner and out again in the short time it took Jenny to wash the stair.

'It's indigestion you'll get,' she said one day, moving aside for him the second time. 'You should carry a piece.'

'Ach no, I come hame for the pleasure o' seeing you.'

She coloured at that, and the next time she was silent, letting him pass. But he caught her waist with his arm, and she saw that his smile was sweet, as her father's had been.

He was tall, too, like her father, with thinning hair and restless eyes. She found herself thinking about him often as she had not done with a man, Kemp, who sometimes spoke to her when she was working.

He said he remembered her from the old days in the ironmonger's.

'Ach, come on, ye mind me fine,' he said persuasively, standing in her way, so that she had almost to wash over his square-toed boots.

She thought it likely enough, although she did not remember him. He was exactly the type that had come about the shop – broad and clumsy like her brother Tom, now married since the war, and living in the Midlands.

Kemp was doing well for himself in the building line. He was a widower and he wanted Jenny to come and clean for him.

'No . . . I couldna.' That was all she would answer, and by and by his sister came to keep house for him.

But every Tuesday and Friday Jenny watched for John Ibbets, twice in a quarter of an hour. Always as he passed he put his hand on her and called some pleasantry to which she replied as he raced up or down the stair.

One evening on her way from work she met him, and he turned back with her. He did not seem to read the papers, or, if he did, he did not tell her what was in them. Neither of them talked very much, but when they reached the close he came inside and kissed her.

It was a melting experience, and he left his mouth where it was till she took her own away. She would have done anything for him.

'Jenny,' he said, his arms still round her, 'Jenny, would you come and clean for us whiles?'

She had to go at night when he was there, because his wife hated women and might do her an injury. It was only once a week, and Jenny arranged for Isa, Jim's wife, to look in and make sure her mother was all right. In return, Jenny kept the children for a night to let Jim and Isa go out.

It was a queer exchange – a night at the cinema for two hours' scrubbing under the eye of a woman who never relaxed. Mrs Ibbets had once been pretty in a dark way, but now she was a wizened creature, with an air of knowing something more terrible than anybody else could imagine. Her husband stroked her shoulders and talked to her continually.

'Ach, Martha, she canny get me when you're here. Nobody can get me . . . d'ye no' ken that, ye daft lassie?'

She would giggle, with a distortion of her face like lightning tearing a small stubborn rock.

Once Jenny asked John Ibbets as he passed up the stair: 'What made her like that?'

He could not stop to answer, for his wife watched at the window, and was always waiting for him behind the door.

On his way down he muttered: 'Once away our holidays . . . a girl . . . there was no harm in it, but she caught us . . . she tried to do hersel' in.'

Jenny knew it was a lie. At least she knew there was more. His mouth was weak like her father's and he did not drink. A woman would always be tortured by doubts if she were fool enough to love him. Unless he were tied to another woman whom he could not love because she was wrong in the mind.

Twenty-five years later the Abercromby drapery stores (three branches) had sold out at a big price to a combine firm. Jenny was still washing stairs.

Her mother had died, and she might have taken a job, but she made no change in her life except that she cleaned at the Ibbets' twice a week instead of once. She took no other cleaning, although Kemp had asked her again and again.

The depression years had hit John Ibbets hard, but he gave Jenny more money than he need have done for two nights' cleaning. She put some of it in the bank, because she thought she might need it if ever . . .

But Mrs Ibbets lived on. People said sympathetically, 'Why doesn't he put her in a home?' But Jenny thought he ought to let her be.

Since the war began again, John Ibbets had been making

good money, but he was a tired man whose voice had dwindled from constantly talking to his wife.

On the twenty-fifth anniversary of the night when he had first kissed her in the close, Jenny finished her scrubbing and left the Ibbets' as usual. He rushed after her, banging the door behind him.

He was sixty-five and she was over fifty, a gaunt woman whom neighbours had compared with an ostrich. But they walked home, and up the long stairs to her house, and were happy together.

The next day she went out with a firm step; the chalky curls on the stair were bright, and she thought she did not need their comfort any more.

She went to start her work, but as she passed the Ibbets' close there was a crowd gathered round. The district had 'gone down' since the days when it was full of teachers and businessmen. The wives of tradesmen and minor clerks were Jenny's employers now, and a few of them stood in a knot about the close.

'It was wee Jean says to me, "*Mammy, what's the funny smell?*..."'

Mrs Ibbets. Mr Ibbets had gone out and left her. Poor man, he'd paid for it now. He came in . . . they must have gone to bed.

She'd got up, turned on the gas, put her head in the oven. He must have been dead beat, he never wakened. The policeman could hardly go in, it was so thick.

'Jenny . . . you're not to take it like that. Aye, it's a shock . . . an' you've lost a good job . . . but there's plenty more. She's better away, poor soul, an' he . . .'

'It was wee Jean says to me, "*Mammy, what's the funny smell?*..."'

She had been alone in her own house for a long time. It must have been evening when she heard feet come up the stair. Heavy feet, but dulled with rubber soles. Then a thumping at the door.

She went at last. He had been turning away, but he came back. It was Kemp, the widower.

'Jenny . . . they're away now . . . you'll be needin' work . . . if there's nobody else before me . . . would you come an' clean for me?'

He was pathetic, knowing he should not have come so soon, but not knowing how else to make sure of her.

Jenny had always been quiet about things. Her brothers had cheated her out of marriage with a man who loved her less than his dignity. She had been left alone to bear the burden of her mother's helplessness. She had been indirectly to blame for the death of the two men she had loved. And now a man was asking something from her.

Gently she closed her door against him.

But a neighbour, coming up the stair half an hour later, saw something black whirling past her and out through the close. Before she could reach it, the missile had rolled away under the wheels of a lorry in the street. She recognized it, crushed as it was. It was Jenny Stairy's bowler hat.

TALKING POINTS

1. The first part of the story deals with the relationship between Jenny's boy friend Peter and her brothers. Outline the main events so as to bring out the drama of this part.
2. The second section builds up to the tragedy of Jenny's father's death. Show how the theme of the first part is woven into the narrative of the second in such a way as to sharpen the tragedy.
3. The third section tells how Jenny became a full-time 'stairy', and unfolds the second tragedy in her life. Consider by what means the author maintains and strengthens a feeling of sympathy for Jenny.
4. Read the opening and conclusion again. Discuss the importance and significance of the hat in the structure of the story as a whole. (Remember – it is not an ordinary hat: it is a bowler.)
5. Was Jenny's life as useless as it might seem at a casual reading of the story? If not, say in what ways you think she was valuable in the lives of others?
6. How far do you think Jenny is symbolic or representative of a kind of woman in every class of society?

Eric Linklater (b. 1899)

SEALSKIN TROUSERS

I am not mad. It is necessary to realize that, to accept it as a fact about which there can be no dispute. I have been seriously ill for some weeks, but that was the result of shock. A double or conjoint shock: for as well as the obvious concussion of a brutal event, there was the more dreadful necessity of recognizing the material evidence of a happening so monstrously implausible that even my friends here, who in general are quite extraordinarily kind and understanding, will not believe in the occurrence, though they cannot deny it or otherwise explain – I mean explain away – the clear and simple testimony of what was left.

I, of course, realized very quickly what had happened, and since then I have more than once remembered that poor Coleridge teased his unquiet mind, quite unnecessarily in his case, with just such a possibility; or impossibility, as the world would call it. 'If a man could pass through Paradise in a dream,' he wrote, 'and have a flower presented to him as a pledge that his soul had really been there, and if he found that flower in his hand when he woke – Ay, and what then?'

But what if he had dreamt of Hell and wakened with his hand burnt by the fire? Or of Chaos, and seen another face stare at him from the looking-glass? Coleridge does not push the question far. He was too timid. But I accepted the evidence, and while I was ill I thought seriously about the whole proceeding, in detail and in sequence of detail. I thought, indeed, about little else. To begin with, I admit, I was badly shaken, but gradually my mind cleared and my vision improved, and because I was patient and persevering – that needed discipline – I can now say that I know what happened. I have indeed, by a conscious intellectual effort, *seen and heard* what happened. This is how it began . . .

How very unpleasant! she thought.

She had come down the great natural steps on the sea-cliff to the ledge that narrowly gave access, round the angle of it, to the western face which today was sheltered from the breeze and warmed by the afternoon sun. At the beginning of the week she and her fiancé, Charles Sellin, had found their way to an almost hidden shelf, a deep veranda sixty feet above the white-veined water. It was rather bigger than a billiard-table and nearly as private as an abandoned lighthouse. Twice they had spent some blissful hours there. She had a good head for heights, and Sellin was indifferent to scenery. There had been nothing vulgar, no physical contact, in their bliss together on this oceanic gazebo, for on each occasion she had been reading Héaloin's *Studies in Biology* and he Lenin's *What is to be Done?*

Their relations were already marital, not because their mutual passion could brook no pause, but rather out of fear lest their friends might despise them for chastity and so conjecture some oddity or impotence in their nature. Their behaviour, however, was very decently circumspect, and they already conducted themselves, in public and out of doors, as if they had been married for several years. They did not regard the seclusion of the cliffs as an opportunity for secret embracing, but were content that the sun should warm and colour their skin; and let their anxious minds be soothed by the surge and cavernous colloquies of the sea. Now, while Charles was writing letters in the little fishing-hotel a mile away, she had come back to their sandstone ledge, and Charles would join her in an hour or two. She was still reading *Studies in Biology*.

But their gazebo, she perceived, was already occupied, and

occupied by a person of the most embarrassing appearance. He was quite unlike Charles. He was not only naked, but obviously robust, brown-hued, and extremely hairy. He sat on the very edge of the rock, dangling his legs over the sea, and down his spine ran a ridge of hair like the dark stripe on a donkey's back, and on his shoulder-blades grew patches of hair like the wings of a bird. Unable in her disappointment to be sensible and leave at once, she lingered for a moment and saw to her relief that he was not quite naked. He wore trousers of a dark brown colour, very low at the waist, but sufficient to cover his haunches. Even so, even with that protection for her modesty, she could not stay and read biology in his company.

To show her annoyance, and let him become aware of it, she made a little impatient sound; and turning to go, looked back to see if he had heard.

He swung himself round and glared at her, more angry on the instant than she had been. He had thick eyebrows, large dark eyes, a broad snub nose, a big mouth. 'You're Roger Fairfield!' she exclaimed in surprise.

He stood up and looked at her intently. 'How do you know?' he asked.

'Because I remember you,' she answered, but then felt a little confused, for what she principally remembered was the brief notoriety he had acquired, in his final year at Edinburgh University, by swimming on a rough autumn day from North Berwick to the Bass Rock to win a bet of five pounds.

The story had gone briskly round the town for a week, and everybody knew that he and some friends had been lunching, too well for caution, before the bet was made. His friends, however, grew quickly sober when he took to the water, and in a great fright informed the police, who called out the life-boat. But they searched in vain, for the sea was running high, until in calm water under the shelter of the Bass they saw his head, dark on the water, and pulled him aboard. He seemed none the worse for his adventure, but the police charged him with disorderly behaviour and he was fined two pounds for swimming without a regulation costume.

'We met twice,' she said, 'once at a dance and once in Mackie's when we had coffee together. About a year ago. There were several of us there, and we knew the man you came in with. I remember you perfectly.'

He stared the harder, his eyes narrowing, a vertical wrinkle dividing his forehead. 'I'm a little short-sighted too,' she said with a nervous laugh.

'My sight's very good,' he answered, 'but I find it difficult to recognize people. Human beings are so much alike.'

'That's one of the rudest remarks I've ever heard!'

'Surely not?'

'Well, one does like to be remembered. It isn't pleasant to be told that one's a nonentity.'

He made an impatient gesture. 'That isn't what I meant, and I do recognize you now. I remember your voice. You have a distinctive voice and a pleasant one. F sharp in the octave below middle C is your note.'

'Is that the only way in which you can distinguish people?'

'It's as good as any other.'

'But you don't remember my name?'

'No,' he said.

'I'm Elizabeth Barford.'

He bowed and said, 'Well, it was a dull party, wasn't it? The occasion, I mean, when we drank coffee together.'

'I don't agree with you. I thought it was very amusing, and we all enjoyed ourselves. Do you remember Charles Sellin?'

'No.'

'Oh, you're hopeless,' she exclaimed. 'What is the good of meeting people if you're going to forget all about them?'

'I don't know,' he said. 'Let us sit down, and you can tell me.'

He sat again on the edge of the rock, his legs dangling, and looking over his shoulder at her, said, 'Tell me: what is the good of meeting people?'

She hesitated, and answered, 'I like to make friends. That's quite natural, isn't it? – But I came here to read.'

'Do you read standing?'

'Of course not, she said, and smoothing her skirt tidily over her knees, sat down beside him. 'What a wonderful place this is for a holiday. Have you been here before?'

'Yes, I know it well.'

'Charles and I came a week ago. Charles Sellin, I mean, whom you don't remember. We're going to be married, you know. In about a year, we hope.'

'Why did you come here?'

'We wanted to be quiet, and in these islands one is fairly secure against interruption. We're both working quite hard.'

'Working!' he mocked. 'Don't waste time, waste your life instead.'

'Most of us have to work, whether we like it or not.'

He took the book from her lap, and opening it read idly a few lines, turned a dozen pages and read with a yawn another paragraph.

'Your friends in Edinburgh,' she said, 'were better-off than ours. Charles and I, and all the people we know, have got to make our living.'

'Why?' he asked.

'Because if we don't we shall starve,' she snapped.

'And if you avoid starvation – what then?'

'It's possible to hope,' she said stiffly, 'that we shall be of some use in the world.'

'Do you agree with this?' he asked, smothering a second yawn, and read from the book:

'The physical factor in a germ-cell is beyond our analysis or assessment, but can we deny subjectivity to the primordial initiatives? It is easier, perhaps, to assume that mind comes late in development, but the assumption must not be established on the grounds that we can certainly deny self-expression to the cell. It is common knowledge that the mind may influence the body both greatly and in little unseen ways; but how it is done, we do not know. Psychobiology is still in its infancy.'

'It's fascinating, isn't it?' she said.

'How do you propose,' he asked, 'to be of use to the world?'

'Well, the world needs people who have been educated – educated to think – and one does hope to have a little influence in some way.'

'Is a little influence going to make any difference? Don't you think that what the world needs is to develop a new sort of mind? It needs a new primordial directive, or quite a lot of them, perhaps. But psychobiology is still in its infancy, and you don't know how such changes come about, do you? And you can't foresee when you *will* know, can you?'

'No, of course not. But science is advancing so quickly —'

'In fifty thousand years?' he interrupted. 'Do you think you will know by then?'

'It's difficult to say,' she answered seriously, and was gathering her thoughts for a careful reply when again he interrupted, rudely, she thought, and quite irrelevantly. His attention had strayed from her and her book to the sea beneath, and he was looking down as though searching for something. 'Do you swim?' he asked.

'Rather well,' she said.

'I went in just before high water, when the weed down there was all brushed in the opposite direction. You never get bored by the sea, do you?'

'I've never seen enough of it,' she said. 'I want to live on an island, a little island, and hear it all round me.'

'That's very sensible of you,' he answered with more

warmth in his voice. 'That's uncommonly sensible for a girl like you.'

'What sort of a girl do you think I am?' she demanded, vexation in her accent, but he ignored her and pointed his brown arm to the horizon: 'The colour has thickened within the last few minutes. The sea was quite pale on the skyline, and now it's a belt of indigo. And the writing has changed. The lines of foam on the water, I mean. Look at that! There's a submerged rock out there, and always, about half an hour after the ebb has started to run, but more clearly when there's an off-shore wind, you can see those two little whirlpools and the circle of white round them. You see the figure they make? It's like this isn't it?'

With a splinter of stone, he drew a diagram on the rock.

'Do you know what it is?' he asked. 'It's the figure the Chinese call the T'ai Chi. They say it represents the origin of all created things. And it's the sign manual of the sea.'

'But those lines of foam must run into every conceivable shape,' she protested.

'Oh, they do. They do indeed. But it isn't often you can read them. – There he is!' he exclaimed, leaning forward and staring into the water sixty feet below. 'That's him, the old villain!'

From his sitting position, pressing hard down with his hands and thrusting against the face of the rock with his heels, he hurled himself into space, and straightening in mid-air broke the smooth green surface of the water with no more splash than a harpoon would have made. A solitary razorbill, sunning himself on a shelf below, fled hurriedly out to sea, and half a dozen white birds, startled by the sudden movement, rose in the air crying 'Kittiwake! Kittiwake!'

Elizabeth screamed loudly, scrambled to her feet with clumsy speed, then knelt again on the edge of the rock and peered down. In the slowly heaving clear water she could see a pale shape moving, now striped by the dark weed that grew in tangles under the flat foot of the rock, now lost in the shadowy deepness where the tangles were rooted. In a minute or two his head rose from the sea, he shook bright drops from his hair, and looked up at her, laughing. Firmly grasped in his right hand, while he trod water, he held up an enormous blue-black lobster for her admiration. Then he threw it on to the flat rock beside him, and swiftly climbing out of the sea, caught it again and held it, cautious of its bite, till he found a piece of string in his trouser-pocket. He shouted to her, 'I'll tie its claws, and you can take it home for your supper!'

She had not thought it possible to climb the sheer face of the cliff, but from its forefoot he mounted by steps and handholds invisible from above, and pitching the tied lobster on to the floor of the gazebo, came nimbly over the edge.

'That's a bigger one than you've ever seen in your life before,' he boasted. 'He weighs fourteen pounds, I'm certain of it. Fourteen pounds at least. Look at the size of his right claw! He could crack a coconut with that. He tried to crack my ankle when I was swimming an hour ago, and got into his hole before I could catch him. But I've caught him now, the brute. He's had more than twenty years of crime, that black boy. He's twenty-four or twenty-five by the look of him. He's older than you, do you realize that? Unless you're a lot older than you look. How old are you?'

But Elizabeth took no interest in the lobster. She had retreated until she stood with her back to the rock, pressed hard against it, the palms of her hands fumbling on the stone as if feeling for a secret lock or bolt that might give her entrance into it. Her face was white, her lips pale and tremulous.

He looked round at her, when she made no answer, and asked what the matter was.

Her voice was faint and frightened. 'Who are you?' she whispered, and the whisper broke into a stammer. 'What are you?'

His expression changed and his face with the water-drops on it, grew hard as a rock shining undersea. 'It's only a few minutes,' he said, 'since you appeared to know me quite well. You addressed me as Roger Fairfield, didn't you?'

'But a name's not everything. It doesn't tell you enough.'

'What more do you want to know?'

Her voice was so strained and thin that her words were like the shadow of words, or words shivering in the cold: 'To jump like that, into the sea – it wasn't human!'

The coldness of his face wrinkled to a frown. 'That's a curious remark to make.'

'You would have killed yourself if – if –'

He took a seaward step again, looked down at the calm green depths below, and said, 'You're exaggerating, aren't you? It's not much more than fifty feet, sixty perhaps, and the water's deep. – Here, come back! Why are you running away?'

'Let me go!' she cried. 'I don't want to stay here. I – I'm frightened.'

'That's unfortunate. I hadn't expected this to happen.'

'Please let me go!'

'I don't think I shall. Not until you've told me what you're frightened of.'

'Why,' she stammered, 'why do you wear fur trousers?'

He laughed, and still laughing caught her round the waist and pulled her towards the edge of the rock. 'Don't be alarmed,' he said. 'I'm not going to throw you over. But if you insist on a conversation about trousers, I think we should sit down again. Look at the smoothness of the water, and its colour, and the light in the depths of it: have you ever seen anything lovelier? Look at the sky: that's calm enough, isn't it? Look at that fulmar sailing past: he's not worrying, so why should you?'

She leaned away from him, all her weight against the hand that held her waist, but his arm was strong and he seemed unaware of any strain on it. Nor did he pay attention to the distress she was in – she was sobbing dryly, like a child who has cried too long – but continued talking in a light and pleasant conversational tone until the muscles of her body tired and relaxed, and she sat within his enclosing arm, making no more effort to escape, but timorously conscious of his hand upon her side so close beneath her breast.

'I needn't tell you,' he said, 'the conventional reasons for wearing trousers. There are people, I know, who sneer at all conventions, and some conventions deserve their sneering. But not the trouser-convention. No, indeed! So we can admit the necessity of the garment, and pass to consideration of the material. Well, I like sitting on rocks, for one thing, and for such a hobby this is the best stuff in the world. It's very durable, yet soft and comfortable. I can slip into the sea for half an hour without doing it any harm and when I come out to sun myself on the rock again, it doesn't feel cold and clammy. Nor does it fade in the sun or shrink with the wet. Oh, there are plenty of reasons for having one's trousers made of stuff like this.'

'And there's a reason,' she said, 'that you haven't told me.'

'Are you quite sure of that?'

She was calmer now, and her breathing was controlled. But her face was still white, and her lips were softly nervous when she asked him, 'Are you going to kill me?'

'Kill you? Good heavens, no! Why should I do that?'

'For fear of my telling other people.'

'And what precisely would you tell them?'

'You know.'

'You jump to conclusions far too quickly: that's your trouble. Well, it's a pity for your sake, and a nuisance for me. I don't think I can let you take that lobster home for your supper after all. I don't, in fact, think you will go home for your supper.'

Her eyes grew dark again with fear, her mouth opened, but

before she could speak he pulled her to him and closed it, not asking leave, with a roughly occludent kiss.

'That was to prevent you from screaming. I hate to hear people scream,' he told her, smiling as he spoke. 'But this' – he kissed her again, now gently and in a more protracted embrace – 'that was because I wanted to.'

'You mustn't!' she cried.

'But I have,' he said.

'I don't understand myself! I can't understand what has happened —'

'Very little yet,' he murmured.

'Something terrible has happened!'

'A kiss? Am I so repulsive?'

'I don't mean that. I mean something inside me. I'm not – at least I think I'm not – I'm not frightened now!'

'You have no reason to be.'

'I have every reason in the world. But I'm not! I'm not frightened – but I want to cry.'

'Then cry,' he said soothingly, and made her pillow her cheek against his breast. 'But you can't cry comfortably with that ridiculous contraption on your nose.'

He took from her the horn-rimmed spectacles she wore, and threw them into the sea.

'Oh!' she exclaimed. 'My glasses! – Oh, why did you do that? Now I can't see. I can't see at all without my glasses!'

'It's all right,' he assured her. 'You really won't need them. The refraction,' he added vaguely, 'will be quite different.'

As if this small but unexpected act of violence had brought to the boiling-point her desire for tears, they bubbled over, and because she threw her arms about him in a sort of fond despair, and snuggled close, sobbing vigorously till he felt the warm drops trickle down his skin, and from his skin she drew into her eyes the saltness of the sea, which made her weep the more. He stroked her hair with a strong but soothing hand, and when she grew calm and lay still in his arms, her emotion spent, he sang quietly to a little enchanting tune a song that began:

> 'I am a Man upon the land,
> I am a Selkie in the sea,
> And when I'm far from every strand
> My home it is on Sule Skerry.'

After the first verse or two she freed herself from his embrace, and sitting up listened gravely to the song. Then she asked him, 'Shall I ever understand?'

'It's not a unique occurrence,' he told her. 'It has happened quite often before, as I suppose you know. In Cornwall and Brittany and among the Western Isles of Scotland; that's where people have always been interested in seals, and understood them a little, and where seals from time to time have taken human shape. The one thing that's unique in our case, in my metamorphosis, is that I am the only seal-man who has ever become a Master of Arts of Edinburgh University. Or, I believe of any university. I am the unique and solitary example of a sophisticated seal-man.'

'I must look a perfect fright,' she said. 'It was silly of me to cry. Are my eyes very red?'

'The lids are a little pink – not unattractively so – but your eyes are as dark and lovely as a mountain pool in October, on a sunny day in October. They're much improved since I threw your spectacles away.'

'I needed them, you know. I feel quite stupid without them. But tell me why you came to the University – and how? How could you do it?'

'My dear girl – what is your name, by the way? I've quite forgotten.'

'Elizabeth!' she said angrily.

'I'm so glad, it's my favourite human name. But you don't really want to listen to a lecture on psychobiology?'

'I want to know *how*. You must tell me!'

'Well, you remember, don't you, what your book says about the primordial initiatives? But it needs a footnote there to explain that they're not exhausted till quite late in life. The germ-cells, as you know, are always renewing themselves, and they keep their initiatives though they nearly always follow the chosen pattern except in the case of certain illnesses, or under special direction. The direction of the mind, that is. And the glands have got a lot to do in a full metamorphosis, the renal first and then the pituitary, as you would expect. It isn't approved of – making the change, I mean – but every now and then one of us does it, just for a frolic in the general way, but in my case there was a special reason.'

'Tell me,' she said again.

'It's too long a story.'

'I want to know.'

'There's been a good deal of unrest, you see, among my people in the last few years: doubt, and dissatisfaction with our leaders, and scepticism about traditional beliefs – all that sort of thing. We've had a lot of discussion under the surface of the sea about the nature of man, for instance. We had always been taught to believe certain things about him, and recent events didn't seem to bear out what our teachers told us. Some of our younger people got dissatisfied, so I volunteered to go ashore and investigate. I'm still considering the report I shall have to make, and that's why I'm living, at present, a double life. I come ashore to think, and go back to the sea to rest.'

'And what do you think of us?' she asked.

'You're interesting. Very interesting indeed. There are going to be some curious mutations among you before long. Within three or four thousand years, perhaps.'

He stooped and rubbed a little smear of blood from his shin. 'I scratched it on a limpet,' he said. 'The limpets, you know, are the same today as they were four hundred thousand years ago. But human beings aren't nearly so stable.'

'Is that your main impression, that humanity's unstable?'

'That's part of it. But from our point of view there's something much more upsetting. Our people, you see, are quite simple creatures, and because we have relatively few beliefs, we're very much attached to them. Our life is a life of sensation – not entirely, but largely – and we ought to be extremely happy. We were, so long as we were satisfied with sensation and a short undisputed creed. We have some advantages over human beings, you know. Human beings have to carry their own weight about, and they don't know how blissful it is to be unconscious of weight: to be wave-borne, to float on the idle sea, to leap without effort in a curving wave, and look up at the dazzle of the sky through a smother of white water, or dive so easily to the calmness far below and take a haddock from the weed-beds in a sudden rush of appetite. – Talking of haddocks,' he said, 'it's getting late. It's nearly time for fish. And I must give you some instruction before we go. The preliminary phase takes a little while, about five minutes for you, I should think, and then you'll be another creature.'

She gasped, as though already she felt the water's chill, and whispered, 'Not yet! Not yet, please.'

He took her in his arms, and expertly, with a strong caressing hand, stroked her hair, stroked the roundness of her head and the back of her neck and her shoulders, feeling her muscles moving to his touch, and down the hollow of her back to her waist and hips. The head again, neck, shoulders, and spine. Again and again. Strongly and firmly his head gave her calmness, and presently she whispered, 'You're sending me to sleep.'

'My God!' he exclaimed, 'you mustn't do that! Stand up, stand up, Elizabeth!'

'Yes,' she said, obeying him. 'Yes, Roger. Why did you call yourself Roger? Roger Fairfield?'

'I found the name in a drowned sailor's pay-book. What does that matter now? Look at me, Elizabeth!'

She looked at him, and smiled.

His voice changed, and he said happily, 'You'll be the prettiest seal between Shetland and the Scillies. Now listen. Listen carefully.'

He held her lightly and whispered in her ear. Then kissed her on the lips and cheek, and bending her head back, on the throat. He looked, and saw the colour come deeply into her face.

'Good,' he said. 'That's the first stage. The adrenalin's flowing nicely now. You know about the pituitary, don't you? That makes it easy then. There are two parts in the pituitary gland, the anterior and posterior lobes, and both must act together. It's not difficult, and I'll tell you how.'

Then he whispered again, most urgently, and watched her closely. In a little while he said, 'And now you can take it easy. Let's sit down and wait till you're ready. The actual change won't come till we go down.'

'But it's working,' she said quietly and happily. 'I can feel it working.'

'Of course it is.'

She laughed triumphantly, and took his hand.

'We've got nearly five minutes to wait,' he said.

'What will it be like? What shall I feel, Roger?'

'The water moving against your side, the sea caressing you and holding you.'

'Shall I be sorry for what I've left behind?'

'No, I don't think so.'

'You didn't like us, then? Tell me what you discovered in the world.'

'Quite simply,' he said, 'that we have been deceived.'

'But I don't know what your belief had been.'

'Haven't I told you? – Well, we in our innocence respected you because you could work, and were willing to work. That seemed to us truly heroic. We don't work at all, you see, and you'll be much happier when you come to us. We who live in the sea don't struggle to keep our heads above water'

'All my friends worked hard,' she said. 'I never knew anyone who was idle. We had to work, and most of us worked for a good purpose; or so we thought. But you didn't think so?'

'Our teachers had told us,' he said, 'that men endured the burden of human toil to create a surplus of wealth that would give them leisure from the daily task of bread-winning. And in their hard-won leisure, our teachers said, men cultivated wisdom and charity and the fine arts; and became aware of God. But that's not a true description of the world, is it?'

'No,' she said, 'that's not the truth.'

'No,' he repeated, 'our teachers were wrong, and we've been deceived.'

'Men are always being deceived, but they get accustomed to learning the facts too late. They grow accustomed to deceit itself.'

'You are braver than we, perhaps. My people will not like to be told the truth.'

'I shall be with you,' she said, and took his hand. But still he stared gloomily at the moving sea.

The minutes passed, and presently she stood up and with quick fingers put off her clothes. 'It's time,' she said.

He looked at her, and his gloom vanished like the shadow of a cloud that the wind has hurried on, and exultation followed like sunlight spilling from the burning edge of a cloud. 'I wanted to punish them,' he cried, 'for robbing me of my faith, and now, by God, I'm punishing them hard. I'm robbing their treasury now, the inner vault of all their treasury! – I hadn't guessed you were so beautiful! The waves when you swim will catch a burnish from you, the sand will shine like silver when you lie down to sleep, and if you can teach the red seaware to blush so well, I shan't miss the roses of your world.'

'Hurry,' she said.

He, laughing softly, loosened the leather thong that tied his trousers, stepped out of them, and lifted her in his arms. 'Are you ready?' he asked.

She put her arms round his neck and softly kissed his cheek. Then with a great shout he leapt from the rock, from the little veranda, into the green silk calm of the water far below . . .

I heard the splash of their descent – I am quite sure I heard the splash – as I came round the corner of the cliff, by the ledge that leads to the little rock veranda, our gazebo, as we called it. but the first thing I noticed, that really attracted my attention, was an enormous blue-black lobster, its huge claws tied with string, that was moving in a rather ludicrous fashion towards the edge. I think it fell over just before I left, but I wouldn't swear to that. Then I saw her book, the *Studies in Biology*, and her clothes.

Her white linen frock with the brown collar and the brown belt, some other garments, and her shoes were all there. And beside them, lying across her shoes, was a pair of sealskin trousers.

I realized immediately, or almost immediately, what had happened. Or so it seems to me now. And if, as I firmly believe, my apprehension was instantaneous, the faculty of intuition is clearly more important than I had previously supposed, I have, of course, as I said before, given the matter a great deal of thought during my recent illness, but the impression remains that I understood what had happened in a flash, to use a common but illuminating phrase. And no one, need I say? has been able to refute my intuition. No one, that is, has found an alternative explanation for the presence, beside Elizabeth's linen frock, of a pair of sealskin trousers.

I remember also my physical distress at the discovery. My breath, for several minutes I think, came into and went out of my lungs like the hot wind of a dust-storm in the desert. It parched my mouth and grated in my throat. It was, I recall, quite a torment to breathe. But I had to, of course.

Nor did I lose control of myself in spite of the agony, both mental and physical, that I was suffering. I didn't lose control till they began to mock me. Yes, they did, I assure you of that. I heard his voice quite clearly, and honesty compels me to admit that it was singularly sweet and the tune was the most haunting I have ever heard. They were about forty yards away, two seals swimming together, and the evening light was so clear and taut that his voice might have been the vibration of an invisible bow across its coloured bands. He was singing the song that Elizabeth and I had discovered in an album of Scottish music in the little fishing-hotel where we had been living:

> 'I am a Man upon the land,
> I am a Selkie in the sea,
> And when I'm far from any strand
> I am at home on Sule Skerry!'

But his purpose, you see, was mockery. They were happy, together in the vast simplicity of the ocean, and I, abandoned to the terror of life alone, life among human beings, was lost and full of panic. It was then I began to scream. I could hear myself screaming, it was quite horrible. But I couldn't stop. I had to go on screaming . . .

TALKING POINTS

1. In the first sequence of the story proper (apart from the introduction) – up to Roger's dive into the sea – the author gives certain clues as to the identity of Roger. Discuss as many of these as you can trace.
2. Describe the stages by which Elizabeth becomes more and more aware of Roger as a seal-man.
3. One of the purposes of this story of the supernatural is to criticize human society. Discuss the views and the 'philosophy' that arise out of the discussion between Elizabeth and Roger just before the 'change' begins to work.
4. If you are interested in science and medicine, you may wish to discuss the significance of such words as psychobiology, adrenalin, and the pituitary gland, and to consider how successful Linklater is in combining science and the supernatural.
5. How much significance can you see in the throwing away of the glasses?
6. How is the metamorphosis of Elizabeth suggested?
7. Re-read the introduction and the ending (which could be described as the prologue and the epilogue). How are the references to Paradise, Hell, Chaos, and Coleridge's question related to the central idea of the story and its title?

Neil M. Gunn (1891-1973)

ART'S WEDDING PRESENT

'There will be great excitement at home,' said Old Hector as he sat on the little knoll, with one eye on the red cow.

'There is,' said Art. 'Morag is dancing about like a hen on a hot griddle, and if she is, Janet and Neonain are not much better, and Mother is ironing. It's no place for a man yonder.'

Old Hector took his pipe out of his mouth the better to enjoy a soft note or two of laughter.

'And Neonain,' continued Art, 'said she was going to get married, and she is only ten past, and when I asked her who she was going to get married to, she said it was none of my business. I told her she hadn't anyone to get married to. Boy, didn't she grow wild then!' declared Art, his eyes dancing.

'She would.'

'She did. You would think,' added Art, 'that a wedding was a great thing.'

'Well,' replied Old Hector, 'it's not a small thing, as a rule. They contrive, one way or another, to make a lot of it.'

The cunning-shy smile came to Art's features and he half looked away. 'Do you think,' he asked, 'that – that women use it to make fools of men?'

'What's that?' asked Old Hector sharply. Then he observed the confused innocence breaking into merriment as Art pivoted on his bare heel, and he inquired: 'Where did you hear that?'

'I heard Father saying it.'

'Did you indeed? He must have been exercised beyond his usual, surely?' —

'He was. The Dark Woman was in and she and Mother were talking round the fire.'

'In that case,' said Old Hector, 'I have some sympathy for your father. He would have had a hard time of it.'

'That's what he said. He said he didn't know his own house.'

'He wouldn't,' agreed Old Hector. 'They would be joking and taking fun out of him.'

'They were,' said Art. 'And then the Dark One said something to Father, and Mother and herself laughed out loud, and Morag gave a small laugh, too, but I didn't catch what it was.'

'It was maybe as well,' nodded Old Hector.

'I would like to have catched it, though,' said Art. 'You don't know what it might have been?'

'How could I,' said Old Hector, 'seeing I wasn't there?'

'Why are you smiling like that, then?' asked Art.

'A man can smile if he likes, surely?'

Art smiled too. 'And do you know what Father said about Duncan?'

'No.'

'He said, "You would think he had a sore head."'

'Ho! ho! ho!' laughed Old Hector.

Art laughed too. 'Is that a good one?'

'Fair to middling,' replied Old Hector with bright eyes.

'Do you actually think,' asked Art, 'that Duncan has a sore head?'

'Oh, I shouldn't think so.'

'But perhaps a man has a sore head when he's going to be married. You never know. He might have.'

'He might, of course.'

'There's something wrong with him whatever. Donul

asked me to ask him last night if his head was any better, and when I asked him he turned on me and gave me a blow that flattened me.'

'Did he indeed? There would be trouble then.'

'There was,' said Art. 'And Mother took his side, and Morag, too, and Janet and Neonain, but Father took my side.'

'And what about Donul?'

'He ran away,' said Art, 'laughing.'

'The rascal!' Old Hector bushed up his whiskers to scratch underneath, but Art saw he was smiling in them. 'It's a difficult time altogether.' Old Hector shook his head. 'It's not often I get lumps in my porridge, but lumps there were this morning.'

'Is Agnes great about the wedding, too, then?'

'Who isn't? Three of our young hens have been named for thrawing. It's nothing but presents, presents, and clothes, clothes.'

'Are you making a present yourself?' asked Art

'Oh, I'll have to give something, I suppose, but it's not much they have left me after many years. All my feathers are gone.'

Art looked at Old Hector's whiskers. Old Hector looked back at Art. Art flushed very slightly and, to change the thought, said: 'They won't be expecting a present from me, will they?'

Old Hector chuckled. 'I doubt if anyone in the two townships will be let off, but the best present you can make is to stay about your home during this difficult time, so that you may do any little thing that's required of you and run a message when you're asked.'

'Why is it always me? It's queer it should always be me who's got to do that,' remarked Art with some petulance. 'There's Donul: he was off the whole day yesterday, and early this morning he was off again, and he said to me – for

I woke up as he was going – he said, "I'll murder you if you try to follow me." It's queer it should always be me.'

'Never you mind,' said Old Hector soothingly. 'You'll one day be fifteen like Donul, and then you can be off, too.'

'You were off yourself,' said Art moodily, giving his friend at the same time a suspicious glance.

'I was only off on a visit or two. At a time like this, many strange things have to be done. Indeed I've got to be busy this very minute,' and he looked far around the countryside as if his knoll were a watch-tower. 'Now you be a good boy, and run off home, and . . .'

But it was all very well. Art no sooner put his nose inside his home than it was shoved out. 'Can't you run away and play yourself?'

With whom was he going to play? The whole world had gone queer and hidden things were on foot. A fellow could see by the look of the earth itself that things were moving in silence.

Art went down to his own secret place behind the little barn, and sure as he came there the idea struck him. Donul and Hamish had gone off to the River to catch salmon! Not to poach in the ordinary way – he could think of that readily enough at any time – but to get salmon for the wedding feast *as a present*!

It was a thought, and two thoughts. Ducks, hens, butter, cheese, bakings, cakes with currants, a side of pork, a leg of mutton, eggs and more hens, from this one and from that, from here and from here, puddings and shivering jellies, little pastries and big pies, things Art now heard of but had never seen, much less tasted. And Donul and Hamish were adding to this communal feast the distinction of salmon!

Art looked about him and saw the cat. He had nothing in the world that he could give even to the cat itself, barring a kick. And he never kicked the cat. It wasn't safe.

The distant River slowly drew him by the nose. The farther

he went on, the more clearly he saw Donul and Hamish actively engaged at the Hazel Pool.

Skirting Old Hector's cottage at a discreet distance, he paused to spy out the land. There was no sign of Old Hector now. Only women and cows and children here and there. The country was deserted.

He slid down into the hollow beyond, and so entered the Little Glen.

In the Little Glen he was all alone, going away off to find the fabled River and the Hazel Pool, and because this fatal mood was upon him and there was no help for it, he wanted to cry. It was hard on him, having to do all this alone. When the cry mounted he took a little run to himself and the tears that came out bounced off.

Presently he noticed that the glen was quieter and more watchful than when he had gone down it before, perhaps because Mary Ann had been with him then.

But the glen itself seemed to have changed, too. There were curious little places which he had not noticed before, and one or two bends which he could have sworn were not in it the last time. And then he observed, on the other side, the small ravine of a burn which issued in a noisy trickle of water. He certainly had never seen *that* before, so he stood and stared at it until it began to stare back. Whereupon he went on, but with the corner of his left eye on the ravine to prevent a surprise, and while he was thus politely not really looking at the ravine, the earth itself bobbed clean from under his foot and he went face first into a ditch. It was the one he had told Mary Ann how to jump.

So he was on the right road, and even if things could be enchanted, as he had heard Donul say before now, they clearly had not been enchanted entirely.

All the same, they had gone a bit strange, and even if Mary Ann —. The thought of her brought up a vision of the foxgloves which she had called the thimbles of the fairy woman – the foxgloves that grew in front of the wild beast's den, which could not be so very far ahead of him now. Art suddenly stopped.

Mary Ann had said it mightn't be a wild beast's den at all, but the house of the little folk who had planted the foxgloves in front of it for a garden. To Art at this moment there didn't seem much to choose between a wild beast's den and a house of the little folk.

Back he couldn't go, and forward his feet wouldn't budge, so he went sideways down to the stream in the glen, crossed it without misadventure, and climbed the opposite slope until at last he drew himself up through a tongue of heather and lay on his belly peering all round.

And it was lucky for him that he did so, for now striding across the moor towards the side which he had just left came three strange men. Even at a distance Art could see that they were dressed like the Ground Officer when he went to meet the Factor on the day of the collection of rents. And if it came to a choice of passing close to these Great Ones of the earth or to the wild beast's den, Art would rather take a chance on the den.

So it was fear mostly that held him where he was, while the strange men strode down into the glen. By the stream they paused, glanced about them, and debated together, one pointing this way and one another. The oldest took off his cap, scratched his head thoughtfully like an ordinary man, then looked towards where Art lay. But if he was expecting Art to move he was disappointed, for Art was beyond movement now. He had a heavy dark-grey moustache. The youngest man took a thin book from an inside pocket, opened it, and kept on opening it until it grew into a large bright sheet which he laid on the grass. They grouped round this, and the young man moved his finger along it, glancing up and down as he did so. They all nodded, and the oldest said loudly: 'I told you so.' When the young man had folded the map and put it back in his pocket, they crossed the stream and moved down until they came to the mouth of the ravine which had not so long before stared back at Art. They now stared at it. They nodded. Then, the youngest leading, they proceeded in single file, silently, stealthily to enter that place.

No sooner were they out of sight, than Art got to his feet and ran on as fast as he could, indeed a little faster, but when he fell he let no yelp out of him now. The next time he fell was from fright at a big black bird that flapped up from below him. As he gazed down the short steep slope, he saw the body of a dead sheep. Where the wool was off its side, the skin was black, and white maggots were crawling over it. A rotten smell attacked his nostrils, and, pushing back his head, he saw, fair across from him on the other side of the small glen, the ravine of the foxgloves and the wild beast's den. He would have run then, but for one infernal circumstance – the roots of the heather above the den breathed out a faint but unmistakable blue smoke.

Art's mind became a whirling place of wild beasts' dens and little houses of fairy folk and legend and dread that set the world itself going up and down and round like the machinery in the meal mill. Then out of the little door, which Art had discovered on the day Mary Ann and himself had set off to find the fabled River, out of the little door that gave entry to the dark den, came the shaggy head of a great beast, and all at once, O torrents of the mountain, it was not a beast's head, but the hairy *oorishk* itself, the fabulous beast-human. There were legends of this human monster that could chill the heart's blood of grown folk. On all fours it came forth, and slowly it reared itself, and looked around, and Art saw, as in a strange and powerful dream, that the *oorishk* was Old Hector.

And Old Hector surely in the living flesh, for who else could scratch his whiskers in that wise and friendly manner while contemplating the heather breathing smoke? But now, like the *oorishk*, Old Hector got down on all fours and crawled in again.

'It's not much,' said Old Hector, as he stood upright in the cave, 'and ten yards up, the smoke disappears entirely.'

'Good for it,' answered Red Dougal, who was switching the froth off a tub of wash. 'You'll believe me now when I said my peat clods were the blackest and best.'

'I believe you,' said Old Hector, smiling. 'You're stoking well, Donul – but go canny. Hold your hand. She'll be coming near it now.' Old Hector lifted a piece of stick and tapped the head of a large enclosed copper pot with a funnel top to it like a chemist's retort.

'Humour her,' chuckled Red Dougal, switching the froth flat. 'The great thing is to humour her first.' His face was blown red and sweating, and charged with hearty mirth and a heavy brown moustache.

Presently Old Hector said to Donul: 'Come here and smell this.'

Donul bent down and smelt the end of a small copper pipe that issued from the foot of a tub. After sniffing once or twice, as though he couldn't believe his own nostrils, he glanced up at Old Hector, saying: 'It's like the scent of roses.'

'The same, but keener,' nodded Old Hector.

'More searching,' said Red Dougal, getting down to have a sniff himself. 'That's the scent of her coming, Donul, boy. Isn't she the lovely one? And when she's kissed you once or twice in the mouth and put her long white arms round you, it's dead to the world you'll be then, my boy.'

Old Hector set a glass jug whose handle was broken under the end of the pipe. And presently there was a crystal drop, another drop, a quick succession of drops, a pause, a trickle in a small gush.

Old Hector smiled as Donul asked him if that indeed was the true spirit.

'Not quite yet,' he answered. 'See!' From the jug he poured

a little of the crystal liquid into a coarse tumbler and added some water, whereupon the whole turned a milky blue. 'She's not clean yet.'

'Is this weak, then?' asked Donul.

'No. This is the strongest of all,' answered Old Hector, 'but impure. This is the famous "foreshot".'

'Is it?' said Donul wonderingly.

'It is,' said Old Hector. 'There's nothing like this in the whole world for taking the heat out of an inflamed part, and it's capital for the rheumatics.'

'Do you hear him?' Red Dougal asked the chastened wash. 'Damn me, do you hear him?'

Donul smiled, his face red from the heat of the fire. He had never cared greatly for Red Dougal, whom he had hitherto considered to be mostly 'all mouth', but now, somehow or other, the mouth was richer, mellower, and even those references to white arms which would normally leave Donul awkward were here less aggressive. Red Dougal was in his element.

'See how she's clearing,' remarked Old Hector, adding water to a fresh drop. And Donul saw that the milky-blue tinge had all but gone. In another minute or two, Old Hector slipped a small cask under the mouth of the pipe, a copper fillter in its bunghole, and fixed it securely in position. 'You can put on your fire now,' he said to Donul.

When Donul had placed the peat clods in a way that gave the greatest flame with the least smoke, Old Hector nodded approval: 'You're coming at it!'

Donul, flushing with pleasure, straightened himself. The crystal liquid was running in a small but even trickle into the cask. The rumble of boiling was in the fat-bellied pot. Donul's eye ran up the pot to the head that narrowed like the head of a retort, bent over, and was continued in a thin pipe that would have stretched a long way had it not zigzagged upon itself in so parallel and compact a pattern that it was contained in little more than half of a gross barrel or tub. Into this tub, near the foot, water flowed through a piece of lead piping from the burn outside, the overflow being drawn away by another piece of piping. The constant supply of cold water about the zigzagged copper pipe, or 'worm', was sufficient to condense the vapour inside the worm as it was forced through from the boiling pot. Donul followed the whole operation and considered it very neat. Suddenly his eye landed on tiny bubbles breaking on the surface of the water in the tub. 'What's that?' he asked.

'Ah, dear me,' said Old Hector, stripping off his jacket, 'she's started leaking again. She's done.'

It was a very old worm, lead-soldered in many places, and when Old Hector had stopped the pin-point leak, he spoke of ancient days. Red Dougal made a seat for himself of five uneven peats; Donul sat on a ledge of flat rock, and Old Hector on an up-ended wort-tub.

'I'll hear you better,' said Red Dougal, 'if we try the new run.'

So Old Hector raised the filler, ran some four inches into the tumbler, and replaced the filler without having spilt a drop.

'No, no, try it yourself first,' said Red Dougal, politely shoving back the proffered tumbler.

Old Hector sniffed, and sniffed carefully, and nodded to himself thoughtfully. 'There's no guff in this,' he said. He smoothed back the left wing, the right wing, above his mouth, and then drew down an open hand with natural dignity over his beard.

'Take off your bonnet,' said Red Dougal solemnly to Donul, as he removed his own.

If only a few drops went into Old Hector's mouth, he pondered them with some care before ejecting them with precision into the heart of the fire, where they disappeared like an outraged devil in a wild flash. 'Ha–a–,' breathed Old

Hector, both out and in. Then he nodded finally. 'She'll do,' he said, and handed the tumbler to Red Dougal.

Red Dougal took two heavy sniffs. 'Here's my best respects to you,' and he took a mouthful. He held it for a little as if he didn't know what to do with it, and then let it down in a gulp.

He tried not to show any choking, took in air noisily, and smiled through a flow of tears. 'Boys, it's a good drop,' he remarked huskily. 'I'll say that for you, Hector. It's – kha-a-a – special.' He handed the tumbler to Donul.

'No, no,' said Donul, embarrassed.

'Taste it whatever,' suggested Old Hector.

So Donul, pleased at that, warily lifted the edge of the tumbler to his mouth.

'She won't bite you!' cried Red Dougal, glowing now and laughing at Donul trying to take a few drops without taking many.

This was a more difficult operation then Donul expected, for he was used only to drinking water, and indeed it seemed there was a lot in his mouth once he got it in. Round his teeth it went, stinging his gums not unpleasantly.

'Let it down like a man,' said Red Dougal.

'Spit it out,' advised Old Hector.

Donul didn't know which to do, and at last did both. When he recovered, he breathed out and in quickly, smiling and wiping his eyes. 'It's burning,' he said, 'but it's fragrant still.'

Old Hector looked upon him and smiled with a benign humour. 'It's young,' he explained. 'It has still about it the innocence of creation.' From the tumbler he swallowed a small drop and nodded. 'Yes. Youth itself, as yet unspoiled. The fragrance is the fragrance of the yellow barley under the sun and of the wild flowers in sheltered hollows. It has not yet begun to get old, Donul. With the days it grows rank a little, going through all the green humours as man himself does. Only in advanced age does it get back the original innocence, with something added besides.' Old Hector took another small sip.

'In all languages,' said Red Dougal, 'it's called "the water of life". Isn't that wonderful?' He winked openly at Donul, with a sideways nod towards Old Hector. 'He thinks himself innocent at this moment. Isn't that wonderful, too?'

'It can be abused,' said Old Hector, 'but then so can life itself. So can everything.'

'It can be dear,' responded Red Dougal, 'and so damn dear that the folk who first made it in history – our folk – can now neither make nor get.' Thoughtlessly he stretched for the tumbler, and added: 'That's why I made up my mind we'd have a drop for Duncan's wedding, supposing the whole heaven of the gaugers came down upon us in small bits. So I persuaded Hector. And was I not right? For he is the last of the great makers. Good health to you, Hector, and long may your worm leak in the right place.'

'Thank you,' acknowledged Old Hector with pleasant grace.

'Kha-a-a,' said Red Dougal, pleasantly. 'He's a fine fellow, your brother Duncan, Donul; an upright, decent lad. And his wedding is a time when a fellow is shy and needs – when he needs —'

'We're all the better of a little gaiety at such a time,' interposed Old Hector. 'Indeed we suffer from the lack of it, and sometimes I see a sadness on the land.'

'Sadness bedam'd, and if so who is to blame for it but ourselves? Isn't that what I have always been telling you? But would you listen to me? Not you! You would always say that everything should be measured by right conduct, by what is fair and just. To hell with that, say I! It should be measured by action. And this is the kind of action I mean. We're *doing* things now: not sitting and talking and grieving over the past.' Red Dougal cocked his eye at Old Hector. 'Would you say our conduct is fair and just, now?'

Old Hector's eyes glimmered thoughtfully.

'Here,' said Red Dougal, 'have a pull at this before you answer.'

'Put it round with the sun,' said Old Hector.

Red Dougal laughed and handed the tumbler to Donul. 'You're not frightened of leading the lad astray?'

'Open trust never led a lad astray,' murmured Old Hector, 'in all my experience. And I am sure of Donul.'

With a warm smile of pleasant embarrassment Donul investigated the liquor curiously and handed the tumbler to Old Hector.

'Now you can speak,' said Red Dougal, 'and I'll try not to interrupt you.'

Old Hector shook his head. 'What I have to say, you already know.'

'Are we deceiving the Revenue?' demanded Red Dougal.

'We are,' responded Old Hector.

'Are we breaking the law?'

'We are.'

'What would happen to us if the three gaugers were to descend upon us at this moment?' pursued Red Dougal.

'Because the largeness of the fine would be far beyond us, you and I would be put in prison for a very long time, but Donul would not be put in prison, for he had not anything to do with this, but only happened to light on us by chance. And you will both remember that story carefully,' said Old Hector.

Red Dougal laughed. 'Have I not cornered you now, hip and beard?'

'Not that I have noticed,' replied Old Hector mildly.

'Haven't I proved you the very fount and origin of law-breaking and all that's wrong?' demanded Red Dougal.

'Law-breaking, yes,' said Old Hector. 'But wrong is a difficult word. Many a day I have pondered over it, but I am not sure that I have found the answer. I only have a feeling about the answer and sometimes I go by that feeling. For, you see, laws are necessary, and to break them is wrong. Yet a law can be wrong.'

'And is a law wrong just because *you* find it wrong?' scoffed Red Dougal.

'Yes,' answered Old Hector.

'But the law that's wrong to you is sure to be right to the other fellow, or it wouldn't be in it. How then?' demanded Red Dougal.

'I still must judge for myself, just like the other fellow. That he may have the power to make me suffer does not, of itself, mean that he is right. It just means that he has the power to make me suffer. But it remains with me to judge for myself the outcome of all the elements and to come to a decision on the matter.'

'What are the elements here? Eh?'

'Many and varied they are,' replied Old Hector. 'This is our old native drink, made in this land from time immemorial. We were the first makers, as you have just said. For untold centuries we had it as our cordial in life, distilled from the barley grown round our doors. In these times, because it was free, it was never abused. That is known. Deceit and abuse and drunkenness came in with the tax, for the folk had to evade the tax because they were poor. The best smuggler in my young days was an Elder of the Church. Before he started making a drop, he used to pray to God, asking Him not to let the gaugers come upon him unawares.'

'I have heard of that,' said Red Dougal. 'Tell me,' he added with a curious look, 'did you put up a few words yourself before we started here?'

'I did,' replied Old Hector, looking back at Red Dougal with his gentle smile.

The laugh that had been ready to come out died inward in Red Dougal, and he looked downward.

'For we do not make this drink to profit by it at the expense of the tax,' proceeded Old Hector. 'We do not sell it. Just as Donul does not sell a salmon he takes out of the River. Nor would we even make it thus for our own use if we could afford to buy it. But we cannot buy it. We are too poor. The men who have made the law have taken our own drink from us, and have not left us wherewith to buy it. Yet they can buy it, because they are rich. I have the feeling that that is not just. I do not grudge them their riches and all it can buy for them.'

'And do you think,' said Dougal, lifting his head, 'that the Sheriff in his court will listen to your fine reasons?'

'I have no foolish notions about that,' replied Old Hector. 'But I am a man whose eightieth birthday is not so far distant, and I had to decide for myself whether my reasons might meet with understanding in a court higher than the Sheriff's.' There was a pause, and Old Hector looked at the fire. 'There is only one thing,' he added quietly.

'What's that?' asked Red Dougal, eyeing the old man

'I should not,' said Old Hector, 'like to die in prison.'

There was a little silence, and upon it fell a small sound. The sound came from outside. It was no more than the rattle of a tumbling pebble, but it might have been the sounding of the Trumpet of Judgement upon bodies grown rigid and faces that stared. There was no more sound. Then sound came again, and came nearer. The low doorway was slowly darkened, and before their awed eyes a small human figure uprose in the dim chamber and gazed at them, and the figure was Art.

'God be here!' exclaimed Red Dougal harshly, and though the unstable peats upon which he sat now threw him on his back, projecting his heels into the air, yet he contrived to stare from the ground.

Because of the brightness outside, Art at first could see nothing but terrifying faces in an infernal gloom, and he began to whimper where he stood.

'Art,' whispered Old Hector at last. 'Who brought you here?'

'Is there anyone outside?' whispered Red Dougal harshly.

Terror mounted to a wild cry in Art, but Old Hector soon had him by his knee, soothing him. And presently to the question, 'Is there anyone outside?' Art managed to answer: 'No.'

'Who brought you here?'

'M-myself.'

'Did anyone see you coming?'

'No.'

'Glory be to God,' said Old Hector.

'Holy smoke, you gave us the fright there! Phew!' breathed Red Dougal.

'How did you know we were here?' asked Donul.

Art at first could not answer, but at last he told how he had set out for the River and how he had seen Old Hector from across the glen.

Relief was such that they were all smiling now as at a miracle.

'All the same,' said Old Hector, 'we ought to have had Hamish posted where I said.'

'If I put him where I did,' replied Red Dougal, 'it's because he can command a better approach from the south, and that's the way the gaugers must come. Surely that's sense.'

Old Hector turned to Art. 'And you never saw anyone?'

'Yes,' replied Art, 'I saw three strange men.'

Red Dougal, who had been twisting round for the tumbler, stopped in his twist like a man struck by lumbago.

When they had got Art's story, Old Hector nodded with finality. 'They'll be here in one hour. They're combing the glen.'

'Some rat has informed on us!' cried Red Dougal. 'Some bloody rat must have given us away!'

'Let us think,' said Old Hector.

'Think, bedam'd! We've got to get the stuff away, and double quick. Come on!'

'It's too late now,' said Old Hector, sitting quietly where he was.

Red Dougal raged, ready to tear asunder and save what he could, but Old Hector arose, saying: 'It's all or nothing. We'll take the chance.'

Red Dougal gaped at him. But Old Hector was very calm now. 'Come outside,' he commanded, and went before them with an empty malt sack. They followed, and he turned to Art. When he had given Art instructions how to climb up and crawl along the ridge a little way until he could command the glen, and how to watch and report back, he concluded, 'Will you do that?' with a smile that in its great trust moved Art profoundly.

Art nodded, his chest thick with excitement and fear, for well he knew now who the strange men were.

'You two,' commanded Old Hector, 'take this sack and bring back on it the rotten sheep yonder.'

'What's the sense —' stormed Red Dougal, but Old Hector turned from him and, gathering a nest of decomposing undergrowth, placed in it a pile of sheep droppings. Whereupon he crawled back into the cave.

For a moment he stood looking about him thoughtfully. It was a natural cave, open parts to the front having been built in with solid turfs on which the heather outside grew naturally. The long narrow vent above he would close with a couple of divots, once he had flapped the smoke away.

After covering Red Dougal's wash, he withdrew the cask, placed a wooden bucket under the pipe, draped a sack over both pipe and bucket, and bunged the cask with its small drop of whisky. Into the fire he fed some of the nest until an acrid stench got him in the throat. Raking out the fire from under the pot, he threw the remainder of the nest upon it, and, in due course, stamped out the red embers until the dry putrid stink choked him. Rolling the small cask before him, he reached the outside air, where he lay for a little, gasping and wiping his eyes.

By the time Red Dougal and Donul came back carrying the sheep on the sack, Old Hector was sitting by the mouth of the leaden inlet pipe which ran underground, wiping his forehead. The mouth of the pipe he had choked with a sod and concealed with accidental boulders. The wild contortions Dougal and Donul were making to turn their noses away from the sheep sent a smile into his whiskers as he got up and guided them to where the entrance of the cave had been. As the carcass landed with a sickly squelch, the two bearers grunted in concert.

There was little fight left in Dougal now, for the aroma from the sheep had set up an internal argument with the fumes from the liquor, but still he gaped combatantly for the entrance which had disappeared under Old Hector's hand. 'I'll have – *hic!* – the cask though, though the heavens – *hoc!*'

'Don't *hoc* here,' commanded Old Hector sternly. 'There's the cask. You and Donul clear up the burn. Collar Hamish. Get home. Quick!'

Donul, who had crossed the burn and was sitting amid the tall withered stalks of the foxgloves, his head between his knees, arose and followed Dougal.

Old Hector looked around, smothered an abrasion here, smoothed a heel-mark there, then took out his knife and cut a hole in the black tough skin of the sheep. Whereupon he retreated hurriedly across the burn, stabbed his knife in the ground to clean it, and climbed until he saw Art, to whom he beckoned.

'Come with me,' said Old Hector, 'and we'll cross over to the other side of the glen.'

This they did, and soon they were lying in the place

from which Art had recently seen his friend emerge like an *oorishk*.

Art had a thousand questions in him now, but Old Hector whispered that even whispering would keep them from hearing. Presently he dug Art in the ribs. 'Do you see my heroes?'

Art could see nothing but an old raven sitting on the cave above the sheep, croaking at another old raven, both looking all round. But in Old Hector's eyes Art saw a primordial mirth so warm that he nestled into it.

Time passed.

'They're a long time,' whispered Art.

'Time is longer sometimes,' whispered Old Hector.

It got so long that it must have stopped, and Art was about to formulate his own view of time when Old Hector's hand came gently on his back and pressed him into the heather.

Art was frightened to look at first. Then through the heather roots he saw the three strange men coming down the off side of the glen. They stopped, they talked together, looking this way and that. The young man took out his map, but the man with the moustache waved an impatient arm and strode on. The young man returned the map unopened to his pocket. They drew near, they paused, and, rounding the last bluff, surprised two ravens that rose heavily, croaking, from a dead sheep.

They looked at the ravens, they stared at the sheep, they went slowly through the withered foxgloves and peered into the water. Then the young one lifted his head sharply and stared at the cave. As if struck in the face, he backed away among the foxgloves, a hand to his nose. By the way he made up the burn, an unmentionable disease might have been after the fibres in his throat. The others followed, but more slowly.

They had not proceeded many yards, however, when the man with the moustache, going last, paused, turned slowly round, and sniffed the air like a stag. Old Hector lay very still now, for this was the only one he feared. Art felt the large hand grip in his back.

The man swung round as if to recall the two who were fast disappearing in front. With a hoarse croak of laughter, one of the ravens circled down and alighted above the sheep. The man gave it one look, then followed the others out of sight.

Old Hector's head drooped among the heather. Art asked him if they would come back the same way.

'No,' answered Old Hector, lifting his head slowly and regarding Art with a profound and tender smile. 'You saved your old friend from prison that time.'

'Did I?' Art was deeply moved.

'You did. And you saved Duncan's wedding present into the bargain. Indeed, I doubt if such a great wedding present as this of yours was ever made before. All that remains now is for you to hold it *as secret as the grave.*'

'*As secret as the grave,*' murmured Art, his heart like to burst with the amount of life and loyalty in it.

From the novel, *Young Art and Old Hector* (1942).

TALKING POINTS

1. In the opening dialogue there is a contrast between the *naiveté* of the boy and the wisdom of the old man. Discuss this introduction, and indicate what you believe to be the more important themes brought out.

2. In the second part of the story – Art's adventures in the Little Glen – the author presents the scene and the events out of the consciousness of the boy himself. Select and comment on details in this part that reflect the boyish mind and that might seem to him particularly striking and dramatic.

3. The core of the story could be taken to be the scene at the illicit still in the cave. Describe some or all of the following:

    (*a*) The apparatus and the procedure.
    (*b*) The testing of the liquor.
    (*c*) The argument on the law against illicit distilling, and Old Hector's 'philosophy'.
    (*d*) Old Hector's plan of campaign against the gaugers.

4. The arrival of the 'strange men' near the cave may be regarded as the final climax of the story. Discuss the way the author presents this climax.

5. Discuss the appropriateness of the title with particular reference to the concluding dialogue between Art and Old Hector.

Lewis Grassic Gibbon (1901–1935)

FORSAKEN

'Eloi! Eloi! lama sabachthani?'

For a while you could not think at all what strange toun this
was you had come intil, the blash of the lights dazzled your
eyes so long they'd been used to the dark, in your ears were
the shammle and grind and drummle of dream-minded slopes
of earth or of years, your hands moved with a weight as of
lead, draggingly, anciently, so that you glowered down at
them in a kind of grey startlement. And then as you saw the
holes where the nails had been, the dried blood thick on the
long brown palms, and minded back in a flash to that hour,
keen and awful, and the slavering grins on the faces of the
Roman soldiers as they drove the nails into the stinking Yid.
That you minded – but now – now where had you come from
that lang hame?

Right above your head something towered up with branch-
ing arms in the flow of the lights; and you saw that it was a
cross of stone, overlaid with curlecues, strange, dreich signs,
like the banners of the Roman robbers of men whom you'd
preached against in Zion last night. Some Gentile city they
had carried you to, you supposed, and your lips relaxed to
that, thinking of the Samaritans, of the woman by the well
that day whom you'd blessed – as often you'd blessed, pitifully
and angrily, seeing the filth and the foolishness in folk, but the
kindly glimmer of the spirit as well. Here even in the stour
and stench and glare there would surely be such folk —

It was wee Johnny Tamson saw the Yid first – feuch! there

the nasty creature stood, shoggling backward and forward alow Mercat Cross, Johnny kenned at once the coarse brute was drunk same as father was Friday nights when he got his money from the Broo. So he handed a hack on the shins to Pete Gordon that was keeking in at a stall near by to see if he could nick a bit orange. *There's a fortune-teller, let's gang and make faces at him!*

You were standing under the shadow of the Cross and the Friday market was gurling below, but only the two loons had seen you as yet. You saw them come scrambling up the laired steps, one cried *Well, Yid!* and the other had a pluffer in his hand, and he winked and let up with the thing, and ping! on your cheek. But it didn't hurt, though you put up your hand to give it a dight, your hand you hardly felt on your cheek so strange it had grown, your eyen on the loon. Queer that lads had aye been like that, so in Bethlehem long syne you could mind they had been, though you yourself never been so, staring at books, at the sky, at the wan long trail of some northing star that led the tired herdsmen home. . . .

Johnny Tamson was shoggling backward and forward two steps below where the sheeny stood, he'd fallen to a coarse-like singing now, trying to vex the foreign fortune-teller:

> *Yiddy-piddy,*
> *He canna keep steady,*
> *He stan's in an auld nichtgoon!*

But Pete hadn't used his pluffer again, he felt all watery inside him, like. He cried up *Don't vex the man!* for something hurt when he looked in those eyen, terrible queer eyen, like mother's sometimes, like father's once. . . . *Stop it!* he cried to young Johnny Tamson.

Johnny Tamson pranced down the steps at that and circled round Pete like a fell raised cat. *Who're you telling to stop?* he asked, and Pete felt feared to his shackle-bone, Johnny Tamson was a bigger chap than him. So, because he was awful feared he said *You!* and bashed Johnny Tamson one in the neb, it burst into blood like a cracked ink-bottle and Johnny went stitering back and couped, backerty-gets into the stall they'd been sneaking about five minutes before, waiting a chance to nick an orange. Old Ma Cleghorn turned round at that minute, just as Johnny hit the leg of the stall and down it went with a showd and a bang.

You saw the thing that happened and heard the quarrel of the loons, understood in a flash, had moved down from the steps of the Mercat Cross, but had not moved quick enough, crash went the stall, and there was the boy Pete staring appalled. As you put your hand on his shoulder he gasped, and looked round: *Oh, it's you!* and was suddenly urgent – *Come on!*

The Yid man wouldn't or he couldn't run, but came loping down the Gallowgate fine, Pete breathing and snorting through his nose and looking back at the stouring market din. Syne he looked at the mannie, and stopt, the street dark: *You'll be all right here,* he said to the mannie, *but they'd have blamed you – they aye blame Yids. Well, so long, I'm away home!*

You looked after the loon and stared round you again at the clorted house-walls of the antrin toun. And then because you went all light-headed you leaned up against the wall of the street, your hand at your eyen as the very street skellacht; till someone plucked at your sleeve. . . .

God damn and blast it, just like young Pete, coming belting against you out in the streets as you were tearing home for your tea: *Father, there's a Yid chap up in the close – with a night-gown on, he looks awful queer. Well, I'm queer myself, I'm away for my tea. Father, I want you to take him home with us – you're aye taking queer folk home.* . . . So here was Pa, hauled up to speak to the Yid – and a damned queer-looking felly at that, fair starving the creature was by his look.

Ay, then, Comrade!

You saw something in his face you seemed to know from far-off times, in a lowe of sea-water caught by the sun, in a garden at night when the whit owl grew quiet, that awful night in Gethsemane when you couldn't see the way clear at all, when you were only blank, dead afeared. Comrade! You knew him at once, with your hand to your head, to your heart, in greeting.

PETER!

Ay, that's my name. This young nickum here thinks you're no very well. Will you come in by for a dish of tea?

So next you were walking atween the loon and Peter down one dark street and along another and up dark twisting stairs. And at one of those twists the light from the street shone on the staircase and through on you, and Peter gave a kind of gasp.

God, man, where was't I kenned you afore?

II

Sick of father and the tosh he piled in the room, books and papers, an undighted hand-press, wasn't room for a quean to do a hand's-turn to get into her outgoing clothes. Mr Redding had called that evening to Jess: *Miss Gordon, come into the office*, in she'd gone, he was fat, the creash oozed over his collar, and she'd kenned at once when he closed the door the thing he was going to do. And he'd done it, she'd laughed, it hurt, the bloody beast. But she didn't say so, he sweated and loosed her, paiching: *We'll make a night o' it, eh, my Pootsy! I'll pick you up in the car at Mercat Cross.*

Oh, damn! She found herself greeting a bit, not loud, Mother would hear her greeting like a bairn as she minded that. But what else was there for a lassie to do, if she liked bonny things and fine things to eat, and – oh, to be hapt in a fine rug in a car and get a good bed to lie on – even if it was beside that oozing creash in the dark, as it had been afore now. Mind the last time? . . . But she couldn't do anything else, she'd her job to hold on to, a lot of use to find herself sacked, on the Broo, and father with work only now and then and the rest of his time ta'en up with Bolsheviks – he'd be in the jail with it ere all was done, and where would his family be then?

She found the dress and scraped her way intilt, angrily, and heard the whisp-whisp of folk coming in at the kitchen door, wiping their feet on the bass and Mother speaking to them low. She tore the comb through her hair and opened the door and went into the parlour, not heeding them a damn. *Ma —*

You knew that face at once, the long golden throat and the wide, strange eyen and the looping up of the brightsome hair, your heart was twisted with a sudden memory, remembering her sorrow, her repentance, once, that night when she laved your feet with tears, how she followed through the stour of the suns and days of those moons when you trekked your men to El Kuds, Magdalene, the Magdalene.

She thought, Oh gosh, isn't father just awful? Another tink brought into the house, a fright of a fool in an old nightgown. If Mr Redding saw him I'd never hear the end. . . . And she looked at the Yid with a flyting eye, but feared a bit, something queer about him, as though she'd once seen him, once long back – that was daft, where could she have seen him? *Mother, where's my crocodile shoon?*

Ma was seating the Yid by the fire, poor creature, he'd been out in ill weather enough in that silly sark-like thing that he wore. He looked sore troubled in his mind about something, the Lord kenned what, men were like that, Ma never bothered about their daft minds, and their ploys and palavers and blether of right, wrong and hate and all the rest of the dirt, they were only loons that never grew up and came back still wanting their bruises bandaged. But she thought the Yid was a fine-like stock, for all that, not like some of the creatures –

feuch, how they smelt! that Peter would bring from his Bolshevist meetings.

Fegs, lassie, can you no see to the crocodiles yourself – or the alligators either, if it comes to that? Peter was in fair a good humour that night, warming his nieves, steeking and un-steeking them in front of the fire. *Your Ma's to see to the tea for me and this comrade here that young Pete met up by Mercat Cross.*

Jess banged over under the big box bed and found the crocodiles there, oh, no, not cleaned, young Pete was a lazy Bulgar, Ma spoiled him, he never did a thing for his meat, there he sat glowering at that Yid, like a gowk, as though the queer creature were some kind of sweetie. . . . Oh Christ, and they've tint the blasted brushes.

She got down on her knees and raxed out the polish, and started to clean, nobody speaking, Ma seeing to the smokies above the fire, Pa warming his hands and Pete just staring, the Yid – Jess looked up then and saw him look at her, she stopped and looked back with a glower of her brows and next minute felt suddenly sick and faint. . . . Oh Gosh, that couldn't have happened to her, not *that*, after that night with Redding? She'd go daft, she'd go out and drown herself if there were a kid—

You could see in this room with the wide, strange lum and those folk who only half-minded you suddenly a flash in the Magdalene's eyes. She was minding – minding you and the days when she joined the band, the New Men you led, while you preached again chastity, patience and love. The Magdalene minding, her eyes all alowe, in a minute she'd speak as Peter had spoken—

Peter said *Those smokies have fairly a right fine guff. Up with them, Ma, I've the meeting to gang to. Sit in about, Comrade, and help yourself. Queer I thought I'd once met you afore – Dottlet, folk sometimes get, eh, ay? Do you like two lumps or three in your tea?*

You heard yourself say *None, if you please,* though this was a queer and antrin stuff put into a queer and antrin drink. Yet it warmed you up as your drank it then and ate the smoked fish the woman Martha served, with a still, grave face (you minded her face in other time, before that birling of dust went past).

Pete thought as he ate up his bit of a smoky. *My Yid chap was famisht as Pa would say. Look how he's tearing into the fish. Maybe he'll help me to plane my bookcase after he's finisht.* And he called out loud, they all gave a loup, *Will you help me to plane my bookcase, chap? You were once a joiner and should do it just fine.*

The loon, you saw, knew you – or kenned only that? *How did you ken that I carpentered?*

— *Och, I just kent. Will you help me? Ma, there's Will coming up the stair.*

Jess got to her feet and slipped into the room, and banged the door and stood biting her lips, feared, but not now so feared as she'd been. If that was the thing that had happened to her she kenned a place where they'd see to it. Ugh, it made her shiver, that couldn't be helped, she'd see to the thing in spite of the Yid. . . . Och, she was going clean daft, she supposed, what had the Yid to do with it all? Something queer as he stared at her? If she vexed over every gowk that stared she'd be in a damn fine soss ere long. In a damn fine soss already, oh Gosh! . . .

Will thought as he stepped in and snibbed the door, Hello, another recruit for the Cause. A perfect devil for recruits, old Pa – wish to God he'd get some with some sense and go. And he sighed, fell tired, and nodded to the man that sat in the queer get-up by the table. Looked clean done in, poor devil in that fancy gown of his, some unemployed Lascar up from the Docks trying on the old fortune-telling stunt. . . .

Of him you were hardly sure at all – the thin, cool face and the burning eyes and the body that had a faint twist as it moved. And then you minded – a breathing space, an hour at night on the twilight's edge when the trees stood thin as pencil smoke, wan, against the saffron sky, in a village you rested in as a train went through, gurling camels with loping tails, and a childe bent down from a camel back, in the light, and stared at you with hard, fierce, cool eyes. And they'd told you he was a Sanhedrin man, Saul of Tarsus, a hater and contemner of the New Men you led.

Will, this is a comrade that young Pete found. My son's the secretary of the Communist cell. Would you be one of the Party yourself?

Will thought, Just like Pa, simple as ever. Poor devil of a Yid, of course he'll say *Ay.* . . . But instead the man looked up and stared, and seemed to think, and syne nodded, half doubtful. *All things in common for the glory of God.*

Pa said *Ay, just that's what I tell Will. But he will not have it you can be religious at all if you're communist, I think that's daft, the two are the same. But he kens his job well enough, I'll say that. Eat up, Comrade, you're taking nothing.*

You thought back on that wild march up on El Kuds and the ancient phrases came soft on your lips as you looked at the bitter, cool face of Saul, and you heard yourself say them, aloud in the room. *All things in common in the Kingdom of God, when the hearts of men are changed by light, when sin has ceased to be.*

Will thought, Queer how that delusion still lasts, queer enough in this poor, ragged devil from the docks. Funny, too, how he said the old, empty words as though they were new and bit and pringled, not the grim, toothless tykes they are. Looked in a funny-like way when he said them, one half-believed one had seen him before. Oh, well, oh hell, couldn't let that pass. Agitprop, even while eating a smoky!

That's been tried and found useless over long, Comrade. Waiting the change of heart, I mean. It's not the heart we want to change, but the system. Skunks with quite normal hearts can work miraculous

*change for the good of men. People who have themselves changed
hearts are generally crucified – like Christ.*

— *Christ? Who is Christ?*

They all glowered at him, Pete fair ashamed, it wasn't
fair the poor Yid should be shown up like that. Ma turned to
the fire again, Eh me, the Jew felly was unco unlearned, poor
brute, with they staring eyen – and whatever had he been
doing to those hands of his? Pa reddened and pushed the oat
cakes over.

*Help yourself, Comrade, you're eating nothing. Never mind
about Jesus, he's long been dead.*

Jesus? What Jesus was this of theirs, who brought that look
of shame to them? Some prophet of antique time, no doubt,
this man named as someone you knew had been named. . . .
Saul's eyen staring with that question in them – neither the
eyen of an enemy nor yet of a frere.

Who was Jesus?

Ma thought, Well, well, and now they'll be at it. Will'll
never get his smoky down at all with all this blether he's
having on hand telling the poor Jew man about Jesus – Eh
me, and the way he speaks, too, right bonny, though no very
decent my mother'd have thought. But that was long syne,
afore you met in with Peter Gordon and his queer-like
notions – scandalized mother off the earth, near, they had! . . .
Will, would you have another smoky?

— *No, Ma, thank you kindly. . . . So that was the way of it,
you see, this Prophet childe started with the notion that men's
hearts would first need changing, to make them love one another,
care for the State – he called it the Kingdom of God in his lingo.
And what happened was that he himself was crucified after leading
an army against Jerusalem; syne, hardly was he dead than his
followers started making a god of him, quite the old kind of God,
started toning down all he'd taught to make it fit in with the structure of the Roman state. They became priests and princes in the
service of the temples dedicated to the dead Jesus, whom they'd made*

a God. . . . And, mind you, that change of heart must have happened often enough to folk when they heard of the sayings of this Jesus. Thousands and thousands changed – but there was no cohesion – no holding together, they put off the Kingdom of God till Eternity: and were tortured and murdered in Jesus' name.

You stared in the bright sharp eyes of Saul and saw now that he had no knowledge of you. Jesus? – many years ago, he had said. . . . And after that last black night, that hour when you cried to God forsaking you, mad darkness had descended again on the earth, on the faces and souls of Magdalene and Martha, Peter and Saul – Peter there with the old, kind smile on his face, his mind far lost in dreams. And those banners you had led up the passes against El Kuds were put away for the flaunting flag of a God – a God worshipped afar in the strange touns.

Ma cried, *Eh, mighty, the poor childe's no well. Lean back a minute; Pete, open that window; Fegs you fair gave me a turn, man!*

III

Jess Gordon came out from the room all dressed, with her crocodiles on, as they tended the Yid. He opened his eyen as she stepped in the room, Gosh, what need had he to look at her like that, as though he both *kenned* and nearly grat? Well, she didn't care, not a damn, she was going out with Redding, she would tell them all that, that greasy Lascar into the bargain. *What's wrong with him, Ma?*

And now you saw she was not the Magdalene – or the Magdalene after two thousand years with the steel of a Roman sword in her heart, sharper, clearer, colder than of yore, not to be moved by glance or touch or the aura of God that you carried from those Bethlehem days as a loon. This was Magdalene from the thousands of years that drummlet and rumblet into the night since the pain tore deep in your wounded feet. . . .

Ma said, *The childe was feeling the heat, just don't vex him and don't stare at him like that, as though he had done you some ill or other. And where are you off to with your crocodiles on?*

— *To meet a chap if you want to know.* Jess dragged her eyen from those staring eyen. (Damn him, he could stare.) *Ta-ta, folk.*

Ta, ta, they called. She turned at the door. *And ta-ta, YOU.* Her look was a knife.

Pa louped up as she banged the door. *What's ta'en the ill-getted bitch the night? Glowering that way at the Comrade here? ... Eh, what did you say?*

You had said only *Peter!* and at that he had turned, for a moment you saw loup into his eyen that love and amazement that had once been his, love and amazement for the leader, not the creed, it died away as he sat down again. And even he you saw now was not the Peter of that other time, weak and leal and kind he had been, but more of the kindness now, little of the love, forsaken of the trust and uttermost belief. No thing in him now you could ever touch except with a cry of despair.

Ma said, *There was nothing to fuss about. Finish your tea, you've your meeting, Pa. Pete, it's time you were off to your bed. Say ta-ta now to the gentleman.*

— *Och, isn't there no time for my bookcase, Ma? All right, all right, ta-ta, chap.*

The mannie looked and said *Ta-ta.* And again something came twisting in young Pete's wame. He looked back, white-faced, from the bedroom door. *Ta-ta. I – liked you awful, you ken.*

— *Hear that?* said Pa. *He's fair ta'en to you, Comrade. Well, I'll need t'away to the meeting, I doubt. You'll be down there, Will?*

— *Ay will I, worse luck. Is the comrade coming?*

You looked from the face of one to the other, the faces of Martha and Saul and Peter, and you saw, no mist now happing your eyen (that mist from past times), they'd no kinship with you. Saul with the bitter face and creed, a leader once for that army you led up the heights to El Kuds, never for that love you had led it with. Looking into his heart with that ancient power you saw the white, stainless soul that was there, but love had gone from it, faith and trust, hope even, only resolve remained. Nothing there but resolve, nothing else that survived the awful torment your name had become. . . . And you saw in the face of Martha even something that was newer or older than you – a cold and a strange and a terrible thing, a mother of men with the eyen of men, facing fear and pain without hope as did Saul, wary and cool, unbannered, unafraid. . . . You shook your head:

No. I maun gang to my hame.

They could never make up their minds what he said next that minute when he covered his face with his hands, afore he went out of the house and their lives. Pa said it was something about some Eliot, Will said the poor Lascar devil had mumbled something or other about the Sabbath.

TALKING POINTS

(The quotation at the beginning of the story is from the Hebrew and means 'Lord, Lord, why hast thou forsaken me?' See Matthew XXVII, 46 and Mark XV, 34.)

1. By the end of the first section we become aware of the method used by the author in running two stories side by side – the first from the consciousness of the biblical figure and the second from the viewpoint of present-day characters. What details in the first two paragraphs suggest the story of the Gospels, and what kind of picture of modern life is sketched?

2. Discuss the 'modern' characters Peter, Jess and Will; and consider how they are linked and associated with the biblical characters the disciple Peter, Mary Magdalene and Saul of Tarsus.

3. Discuss the big climax that the author builds up to in his second section, and consider the effect here of the repeated question, 'Who was Jesus?'

4. Read the final section again and consider how the title of the story becomes more appropriate as the ending approaches. What, briefly, is the great theme that is re-stated here?

5. Consider Lewis Grassic Gibbon's individual way in handling language. What effect is gained by his use of a direct penetrating style in re-telling the story of Christ?

6. What general commentary does this story make on the nature of man's reaction to the gospel of loving your neighbour?

Appendix

THE ART OF THE SHORT STORY

For some people, short story writing is a preliminary canter
to the writing of a novel; for others the short story is a literary
form in its own right quite different in aim and technique
from the novel. There is no doubt that the short story form
calls for skill in compression, and speed in development,
description, and characterization; but then a writer may
conceivably develop that compression and economy of means
and still incorporate something of the variety of incident and
character and the extension of the viewpoint that are marks of
the novel. Eric Linklater in 'Goose Girl' and Fred Urquhart
in 'The Last G.I. Bride Wore Tartan' provide good examples
of the short story as miniature novel; and in the nineteenth
century A. S. Pushkin and Leo Tolstoy, to mention but two
Russian writers, tended also to use a wide canvas in their
stories. On the other hand Gogol and Chekhov exemplify
the more concentrated kind of story out of which a strong
and unified impression of a character or situation emerges.
Of all the nineteenth-century writers, perhaps Guy de
Maupassant best illustrates the powers of emotion and satirical
commentary of which the short story is capable. In nineteenth-
century Scotland, Scott and Stevenson produced the most
accomplished short stories: the strength of their work owed
something to a kind of ballad directness and folk drama.
'Wandering Willie's Tale' and 'Thrawn Janet' take some
time to unfold, but there is no dissipation of means, no mere
duplication or proliferation of narrative. There is something
of the novel technique in description and character drawing

in the portraits of Steenie and Soulis; but the inexorable movement to climax and coda is the outstanding characteristic – a
characteristic that seems to us to be a vital one for the short
story as separate literary genre.

The short story has been likened to the poem: each may
be based on a single experience, an expanded thought, an
incident leading to a commentary explicit or implicit; and
each may try to give a glimpse into life, into a personal
situation, without suggesting finality. Perhaps H. E. Bates,
A. E. Coppard, Bill Naughton, and Ted Hughes best represent
the slice-of-life story with its realism sometimes reaching out
to or dissolving into a kind of romanticism; and certainly
Chekhov is the outstanding example of a writer who, without
stressing beginning and end, yet succeeded in giving subtle
shape to his stories and plays. On the other hand there is a
fascination about the deliberately patterned story that has a
surprise ending or a twist at the end; in the best of tales this
ending serves to sharpen the critical commentary. Maupassant's 'La Parure', Somerset Maugham's 'The Verger' and
Stacy Aumonier's 'Miss Bracegirdle Does Her Duty' are all
carefully constructed stories that contain compassionate or
satirical commentaries on the human scene.

Form in art is closely linked with purpose or aim. Basically
the story is meant to entertain, to enable us to relax, to take
us from ourselves while we follow the fortunes or misfortunes
of others. Classical myths, medieval romances, epics, ballads,
narrative poems are the material out of which the short story
evolves. From a short story we are justified in expecting some
kind of narrative, a series of incidents, with one or more
climaxes or revelatory points. From the story too we are
bound to have at least one character on whom the action
centres. If the emphasis is on a quality, then the work tends to
be a character-story. Some writers have been so preoccupied
with psychological problems, so bewitched by the analysis of
conscious or unconscious thought, that they produce little

narrative in the normal sense. There must be a point at which fiction becomes case history, the tale becomes refined analysis of the working of the mind; yet it would be wrong to lay down any hard and fast rule and say that the short story must relate a series of connected incidents in chronological order.

For one thing we are all interested in the flash-back technique which enables a writer to start at the end or in the middle; and indeed, in playing about with time, the writer can enrich the scope and extend the range – social and psychological – of his short story. Again if the writer is concerned with understanding human dilemmas or awakening sympathy, he will not play the omniscient author but tell the story out of the consciousness of his characters. Of modern Scottish authors Lewis Grassic Gibbon and Neil Gunn have best succeeded in doing this. There is more time in a novel than in a short story to move from one angle to another, from one point of view to another; yet a carefully worked-out pattern can do precisely this and make the story more effective and relevant as a human document.

It would be wrong also to assume that a story must be about the adventures of a person or persons, although this is a basic form. (The early form of the novel, stemming perhaps from medieval romances, was the 'picaresque' or rogue novel that traced the adventures of a vagabond: Smollett's *Humphrey Clinker* and Fielding's *Tom Jones* are the best examples in English.) A story can be about a place – a mountain or a street; it can be about a text which enshrines a well-known legend or parable, and the shaping of this becomes as intricate as the shaping of a piece of music. There may be a counterpointing of one story with another; there may even be three stories emerging from or revolving within the original. The best example of this kind of intricate pattern is the George Mackay Brown story 'A Treading of Grapes'; but we notice also that Iain Crichton Smith enjoys counterpointing one story with another in 'Survival without Error'. On the other hand the short story may appear to be aimless and shapeless and yet by a kind of humorous string-development such as one finds, for example, in Dylan Thomas's 'A Story', the thing lives and delights us. The stories of Thomas, Saroyan and Wolfgang Borchert ('Thithyphuth') remind us that the humorous story has its own shape and logic.

The art of the short story is an infinitely varied one. The skill may lie in the steady build-up of straightforward narrative within which there are references to setting and character qualities; or the skill may lie in the juxtaposition of an apparently reasonable or comprehensible story-line with a strange twist, a scarcely understandable ending; or it may lie in the apparent shapelessness that unfolds comedy. Time may not be treated chronologically and may in fact be counterpointed with eternity. An apparently realistic or contemporary setting may expand into the romantic future or a timeless vision. Eric Linklater does precisely this in 'Kind Kitty' – his study of a dissolute *cailleach* (old woman) who become a near saint. Or the story may be concerned with revealing the aspirations and deep human qualities of the most ordinary people – as in 'Jenny Stairy's Hat' by Margaret Hamilton. The more recent stories of George Mackay Brown and Iain Crichton Smith are experiments in using musical technique in the short story – in weaving two or more stories together as tunes or *leitmotifs*.

It is practically impossible to analyse the art of the short story, but pattern is in it, a feeling for the human situation is in it, wit and humour are in it, and poetry is in it. Poetry is a dangerous word to use; but it is true to say that a good short story is akin to a poem. Not only is there concentration and compassion, directness and insight: there is that kind of illumination that comes from setting fire to a series of incidents or from putting the flame of life into a character or from sparking together two or more forces or characters. The short story tells a story, that is true; but even the simplest of tales have that quality of delight and wisdom that comes when the author is handling his materials in a creative, experimental, and dynamic way.

R.M.

J.T.L.